Edward S. Rand

The Rhododendron

Volume 1

Edward S. Rand

The Rhododendron
Volume 1

ISBN/EAN: 9783337380786

Printed in Europe, USA, Canada, Australia, Japan

Cover: Foto ©Andreas Hilbeck / pixelio.de

More available books at **www.hansebooks.com**

THE RHODODENDRON

AND

"AMERICAN PLANTS."

A TREATISE ON THE CULTURE, PROPAGATION, AND SPECIES OF THE RHODODENDRON;

WITH

CULTURAL NOTES UPON OTHER PLANTS WHICH THRIVE UNDER
LIKE TREATMENT, AND DESCRIPTIONS OF SPECIES AND
VARIETIES; WITH A CHAPTER UPON HERBACEOUS
PLANTS REQUIRING SIMILAR CULTURE.

BY

EDWARD SPRAGUE RAND, JR.,

AUTHOR OF "FLOWERS FOR THE PARLOR AND GARDEN;" "GARDEN FLOWERS;"
"BULBS;" "SEVENTY-FIVE FLOWERS."

BOSTON:
LITTLE, BROWN, AND COMPANY.
1871.

CAMBRIDGE:

PRESS OF JOHN WILSON AND SON.

TO

HENRY WINTHROP SARGENT

AND

II. HOLLIS HUNNEWELL,

TO WHOM AMERICAN HORTICULTURE IS SO LARGELY INDEBTED,
AND WHO FULLY APPRECIATE THE BEAUTIES OF

" American Plants,"

THIS VOLUME IS CORDIALLY INSCRIBED.

INTRODUCTION.

THE object of the present volume is to introduce to popular notice a class of plants which, in England, forms one of the most attractive ornaments of the garden. They are commonly known as " American Plants; " as the earliest known Rhododendrons, the Kalmias, and some of the Azaleas, are natives of this continent. The name has, however, been extended to embrace many other plants that require the same general culture, but which are not indigenous to America.

It is a singular and most unaccountable fact that these plants are in this country but little known in cultivation.

The hillsides, from Massachusetts to Virginia, are glorious masses of the Mountain Laurel (Kalmia); and all through the Middle States, and up the slopes of the Alleghanies, we find thousands of acres of the Rose Bay, or " Great Laurel " (Rhodo-

dendron). Yet seldom is a plant of either to be
found in the garden ! There is a popular belief that
these plants " cannot be cultivated."

In spring we eagerly buy the spicy blossoms of
the May Flower (Epigæa), yet never think we
may have it blooming in perfection in our shrubberies.

Popular opinion says it "cannot be grown in
gardens;" and there we rest, without trying the
experiment.

To show that these plants can be grown as easily
as any others is the purpose in the following pages.

The species we may find wild in our woods are
beautiful enough to merit every attention, but we
are by no means limited to these.

The skill of the hybridist, exercised during a score
of years, has created a wealth of floral beauty in
Rhododendrons and Azaleas.

We may have masses of bloom of almost any
color and shade, and combinations and contrasts
innumerable.

To those who have seen the magnificent displays
of these plants at Wodenethe, the charming resi-
dence of H. W. Sargent, or at Wellesley, the magnificent estate of H. Hollis Hunnewell, no word of
ours in praise of their beauty will be needed.

In our own culture, at Glen Ridge, we have not
been unsuccessful; and although our experience is

limited to the past ten years, the results have been so eminently satisfactory as to excite most sanguine hopes for the future.

Our collection of hybrid varieties of Catawbiense Rhododendrons is probably larger than any in the country, and is yearly largely increased for the purpose of experimenting as to their hardiness.

These plants are attractive at all seasons: in flower they are magnificent, in foliage they excel any evergreen.

They can be grown as easily as lilacs, and bloom quite as freely.

In the arrangement of the following pages, Part I. is purely cultural; Part II. comprises a list of the species of Rhododendron, and also a selection of hybrid Catawbiense varieties. To give a full list of these latter would be almost impossible: some English catalogues contain hundreds of varieties, and often but very few of these will be common to any two catalogues.

We have in every case, where possible, referred to a colored illustration of the flower, where one was to be found in any book generally accessible; and have, in the list of books quoted, stated where in this vicinity they could be found.

Part III. treats of Azaleas, Kalmias, and other plants which resemble Rhododendrons, and thrive under similar culture. This list has been extended to include many plants not generally known, and seldom found in gardens. Of most of these we write from experience, and can urge their cultivation. Many are low-growing, and suited for an undergrowth in shrubberies, or as a covering for the surface soil in Rhododendron-beds.

All are very desirable, and, if not to be obtained in this country, can be easily imported with but little expense.

In Part IV. we have given brief descriptions of plants which grow well in Rhododendron-beds.

We would strongly urge their cultivation, as they add much to the attractions of the shrubbery; and thus we are enabled to grow many botanical treasures which never find place in the herbaceous border.

This chapter is, however, only a condensation of a portion of a volume on "Herbaceous Plants," which we hope soon to lay before the public.

To all who would obtain large floral results, with but little effort, we would say: "Grow Rhododendrons, and other American Plants; they are always beautiful, pleasing alike in evergreen foliage and in gorgeous bloom."

GLEN RIDGE, *February*, 1871.

CONTENTS.

PART I.

CULTURE OF THE RHODODENDRON.

CHAPTER I.

CHAPTER II.

CHAPTER III.

CHAPTER IV.

PART II.

DESCRIPTION OF THE RHODODENDRON.

Rhododendron ponticum and varieties. Rhododendron maximum and varieties. R. dauricum. R. californicum. R. arboreum and varieties. R. albiflorum. R. anthopogon. R. campanulatum. R. caucasicum and varieties. R. chrysanthum. R. punctatum. R. hirsutum. R. ferrugineum. R. lapponicum. R. kamtschaticum. R. chamæcistus. Sikkim Rhododendrons. R. Dalhousiæ. R. barbatum. R. lancifolium. R. Wallichii. R. Campbelliæ. R. Roylii. R. cinnabarinum. R. elæagnoides. R. argenteum. R. Falconeri. R. vaccinioides. R. niveum. R. obovatum. R. lepidotum. R. Aucklandii. R. Thomsoni. R. pendulum. R. pumilum. R. Hodgsoni. R. lanatum. R. glaucum. R. Maddeni. R. triflorum. R. setosum. R. Edgeworthi. R. æruginosum. R. salignum. R. ciliatum. R. fulgens. R. nivale. R. virgatum. R. Wightii. R. camelliæflorum. R. candelabrum. R. campylocarpum. R. Nilagiricum. R. formosum. R. Gibsoni. R. javanicum. R. citrinum. R. jasminiflorum. R. Championæ. R. Farreræ. R. Metternichi. R. album. R. Batemani. R. blandfordianum. R. Boothii. R. Brookianum. R. calophyllum. R. grande.

PART III.

OTHER AMERICAN PLANTS.

PLANTS THRIVING UNDER SIMILAR CULTURE WITH RHODO-
DENDRONS, COMMONLY KNOWN AS "AMERICAN PLANTS."

I. The Azalea, culture and species of. — II. The Rhodora. —
III. The Loiseleuria. — IV. The Kalmia. — V. The Ledum.
— VI. The Leiophyllum. — VII. The Menziesia. — VIII.
The Phyllodoce. — IX. The Calluna. — X. The Gypsocallis.
— XI. The Cassiope. — XII. The Arctostaphylos. — XIII.
The Epigæa. — XIV. The Gaultheria. — XV. The Chio-
genes. — XVI. The Linnæa. — XVII. The Mitchella. —
XVIII. The Empetrum. — XIX. The Vaccineum. — XX.
The Leucothoe. — XXI. The Cassandra. — XXII. The
Zenobia. — XXIII. The Andromeda. — XXIV. The

PART IV.

HERBACEOUS PLANTS ADAPTED FOR CULTURE IN RHODODENDRON-BEDS.

L I S T

OF

ILLUSTRATED BOTANICAL WORKS REFERRED TO.

Abbreviations.

Bos. Athæ. . . . . Library of Boston Athenæum.
Bos. Pub. Lib. . . . Library of City of Boston.
Bos. Nat. His. Soc. . Library of Boston Society of Natural History.
E. S. R. Jr. . . . . Library of Edw. S. Rand, Jr.
Mass. Hort. Soc. . . Library of Massachusetts Horticultural Society.
Har. Col. . . . . . Library of Harvard College.

And. Rep. . . . . . Andrews, The Botanist's Repository.
London, 1797–1811. 10 vols. 4to.
Col. Pl. 1–664.
Lib. E. S. R. Jr.

Barton, Fl. . . . Barton, A Flora of North America.
Philadelphia, 1821–23. 3 vols. 4to.
Col. Pl. 1–106.
Lib. E. S. R. Jr.; Bos. Athæ.

Barton, Med.. . . Barton, Medical Botany of the
United States. Philadelphia, 1817–
18. 2 vols. 4to. Col. Pl. 1–50.
Lib. Mass. Hort. Soc.; Lib. E. S. R.
Jr.; Bos. Athæ.

Bax. Brit. Bot. . . Baxter, British Phænogamous Botany. London, 1834–43. 6 vols. 8vo. Col. Pl. 1–509.
Lib. Mass. Hort. Soc. and E. S. R. Jr.

Big. Med. . . . . . Bigelow, American Medical Botany. Boston, 1817–20. 3 vols. 4to. Col. Pl. 1–60.
Lib. E. S. R. Jr.; Lib. Bos. Nat. His. Soc.; Bos. Athæ.

Bot. Mag. . . . . . Curtis, Botanical Magazine. London, 1783–1871. 96 vols. 8vo.
Series I.: vols. 1–53.
    ,,   II.: vols. 53–70.
    ,,   III.: vols. 71–96 and con.
Col. Pl. 1–5877.
Lib. Mass. Hort. Soc. and E. S. R. Jr.; Lib. Bos. Nat. His. Soc.; Bos. Athæ.; Bos. Pub. Lib.; Har. Col.

Bot. Reg. . . . . . Edwards, The Botanical Register. London, 1815–47. 33 vols. Royal 8vo.
Vols. 1–23. Col. Pl. 1–2014.
Vol. 24. 1838. Col. Pl. 1–68.
Vol. 25. 1839. ,, ,, 1–69.
Vol. 26. 1840. ,, ,, 1–71.
Vol. 27. 1841. ,, ,, 1–70.
Vol. 28. 1842. ,, ,, 1–69.
Vol. 29. 1843. ,, ,, 1–66.
Vol. 30. 1844. ,, ,, 1–67.
Vol. 31. 1845. ,, ,, 1–69.
Vol. 32. 1846. ,, ,, 1–69.
Vol. 33. 1847. ,, ,, 1–70.

In all . . . 2702 plates.
Lib. of Mass. Hort. Soc. and E. S. R. Jr.; and Bos. Nat. His. Soc.; Bos. Pub. Lib.

ENG. BOT. . . . . . SMITH & SOWERBY, English Botany.
London, 1790–1814. 36 vols. 8vo.
Col. Pl. 1–2592.
Supplement by Hooker. London,
1831–55. 5 vols. Col. Pl. 2593–
2995.
Lib. Mass. Hort. Soc.
New Edition, arranged according to
natural system. London, 1863–70.
Vols. 1–10, and continued. Royal
8vo. Col. Pl. 1–1545.
Lib. E. S. R. Jr.

FL. DES SER. . . . VAN HOUTTE, Flore des Serres et
des Jardins de l'Europe. 18 vols.
Gand, 1845–1871, and continued.
Col. Pl. 1–1926.
Lib. Mass. Hort. Soc. and E. S. R. Jr.

FL. MAG. . . . . . MOORE, The Floral Magazine. Lon-
don, 1861–71. 9 vols. 8vo. Col.
Pl. 1–512, and continued.
Lib. Mass. Hort. Soc. and E. S. R. Jr.

FLORIST . . . . . The Florist. 1st Series. London,
1848–62. 14 vols. 12mo. Col. Pl.—
2d Series. London, 1862–67. 6 vols.
Royal 8vo. 144 Col. Pl. — 3d
Series. 1868–71, and continued.
3 vols. Royal 8vo. 36 Col. Pl.
Lib. Mass. Hort. Soc. and E. S. R. Jr.

HEN. ILLUS. BOU. . HENDERSON, The Illustrated Bouquet. London, 1857–64. 3 vols.
4to. Col. Pl. 1–85.
Lib. Mass. Hort. Soc.

HOOK. EX. . . . . HOOKER, Exotic Flora. Edinburgh,
1823–27. 3 vols. 8vo. Col. Pl.
1–232.
Lib. Mass. Hort. Soc.; Bos. Nat.
His. Soc.; Bos. Pub. Lib.

Hook. Fl. Bor. Am. . Hooker, Flora Boreali-Americana.
London, 1833–40. 2 vols. 4to.
Pl. 1–238.
Lib. E. S. R. Jr.; Bos. Nat. His.
Soc.; Bos. Pub. Lib.; Bos. Athæ.

Hook. Rhod. . . . Joseph D. Hooker, The Rhododendrons of Sikkim Himalaya. Lon-
don, 1849–55. 1 vol. folio. Pl. 1–30.
Lib. Mass. Hort. Soc. and E. S. R.
Jr.; Bos. Nat. His. Soc.

Illus. Hort. . . . Lemaire, L'Illustration Horticole.
Gand, 1854–71. 17 vols. 8vo.
1st Series, vols. 1–10, 1854–63.
Col. Pl. 1–386. 2d Series, vols.
11–17, and continued. Col. Pl.
387–550.
Lib. Mass. Hort. Soc. and E. S. R. Jr.

Lem. Jar. . . . . Lemaire, Le Jardin Fleuriste. Gand,
1851–54. 4 vols. 8vo. Col. Pl.
1–430.
Lib. E. S. R. Jr.

Lodd. Cab. . . . . Loddige, The Botanical Cabinet.
London, 1818–33. 20 vols. L. P.
square 8vo. Col. Pl. 1–2000.
Lib. E. S. R. Jr.; Lib. Har. Col.;
Bos. Pub. Lib.

Maud. Bot. . . . Maund, The Botanist. London, 1839–
44. 5 vols. L. P. small 4to. Col.
Pl. 1–250.
Lib. E. S. R. Jr.

Mich. Arb. . . . . Michaux, The North American
Sylva. Philadelphia, 1857. 3 vols.
L. P. Royal 8vo. Col. Pl. 1–156.
Continued by Nuttall, 3 vols. uni-
form with above. Col. Pl. 1–121.
Lib. E. S. R. Jr.; Mass. Hort. Soc.;
Bos. Soc. Nat. His.; Bos. Pub.
Lib.; Bos. Athæ.

PAX. FL. G. . . PAXTON, The Flower Garden. London, 1850–53. 3 vols. 4to. Col. Pl. 1–106.
Lib. Mass. Hort. Soc. and E. S. R. Jr.

PAX. MAG. . . . . PAXTON, Magazine of Botany. London, 1834–49. 16 vols. 8vo. Col. Pl. 48 in each vol., in all 768.
Lib. Mass. Hort. Soc. and E. S. R. Jr.; Bos. Athæ.

PURSH, FL. . . PURSH, Flora Americæ Septentrionalis. London, 1814. 2 vols. 8vo. 24 plain and colored plates.
Lib. E. S. R. Jr.

REV. HORT. . . Revue Horticole. Paris, 1855–71, and continued. 16 vols. 1855–65, 24 colored plates in each vol.; 1865–71, 52 colored plates in each vol.
Lib. Mass. Hort. Soc. and E. S. R. Jr.

SIEB. FL. JAP. . . SIEBOLD, Flora Japonica. 2 vols. folio. Vol. I. Lugd. Bat. 1835–44. Pl. 1–127.
Lib. Mass. Hort. Soc. and E. S. R. Jr. Vol. II. do. 1870. Pl. 128–150.
Lib. Mass. Hort. Soc.

STEPH. MED. STEPHENSON, Medical Botany. London, 1834–36. 3 vols. 8vo. Col. Pl. 1–185.
Lib. E. S. R. Jr.

SWEET, FL. G. . SWEET, The British Flower Garden. London, 1823–29. 3 vols. 8vo. Col. Pl. 1–300. — 2d Series. London, 1831–38. 4 vols. 8vo. Col. Pl. 1–452.
Lib. Mass. Hort. Soc. and E. S. R. Jr.; Bos. Pub. Lib.

SWEET, ORN. G. . . SWEET, The Ornamental Flower Garden. London, 1854. 4 vols. 8vo. Col. Pl. 288.
Lib. E. S. R. Jr.

TORR. N. Y. . . . TORREY, Flora of the State of New York. Albany, 1843. 2 vols. 4to. Col. Pl. 1-161.
Lib. E. S. R. Jr.

WIGHT, IC. . . . . WIGHT, Icones Plantarum Indiæ Orientalis. Madras, 1838-53. 6 vols. 4to. Pl. 1-2101.
Lib. Mass. Hort. Soc. and E. S. R. Jr.

WIGHT, ILL. . . . WIGHT, Illustrations of Indian Botany. Madras, 1838-48. 2 vols. 4to. Col. Pl. 1-182.
Lib. E. S. R. Jr.

WOOD. MED. . . . WOODVILLE, Medical Botany. London, 1832. 5 vols. 4to. Vols. 1-4, Col. Pl. 1-274; vol. 5, Col. Pl. 1-39.

PART I.

CULTURE OF THE RHODODENDRON.

THE RHODODENDRON.

PART I.

CULTURE OF THE RHODODENDRON.

CHAPTER I.

PREPARATION OF THE SOIL.

THE highest aim in the cultivation of a plant is to grow it in such a manner as to attain the most perfect results. Careless culture, though sometimes partially successful, in most cases brings disappointment.

To grow a plant well, requires a study of its peculiarities, and adaptations to suit them.

There are, in plant culture, certain general rules which can never be transgressed: these are usually understood. There are also many lesser points to be observed, too often wholly ignored, but they contribute greatly to success, which is often in direct ratio with their observance.

The Rhododendron requires careful culture. To those who are not willing to give it, we say, Do not attempt to grow Rhododendrons; yet, so doing, you give up one of the most beautiful of plants, one of the most glorious ornaments of the garden, which more richly repays the care it requires than any plant we can mention. Let us not, however, be misunderstood. After the first planting, that being well done, *the Rhododendron requires less attention than any other plant;* but this preparation of the soil is of primary importance.

We are aware that in this we differ from some cultivators, who maintain that Rhododendrons will do well in any garden soil. This is true in a degree; for the plants will live, grow, and bloom in any deep loam not containing lime; but they will not, under this culture, attain the highest perfection, either of foliage or flower.

The Rhododendron is a native of swamps, of shady mountain sides, or of deep ravines, usually on the banks of mountain streams. In these situations it forms impenetrable thickets or jungles, the plant attaining great size, the boughs bending down and rooting by natural layers, producing in the Middle and Southern States the nearest approach our flora can make to a tropical jungle.

Some species are found in mountain swamps, occasionally in high latitudes, but always in moist situations.

The natural habitat of the plants gives us the first requisite for their successful culture,—a moist soil. The roots of all the species, except perhaps some of the epiphytal kinds of the Himalaya Mountains, are fine and hair-like; and drought is certain death.

In a wild state, they grow most luxuriantly in a peaty loam, formed by the débris of decayed vegetable matter, such as wood and leaves, with an admixture of disintegrated rocks, and generally in a shady situation. These conditions we must, in a measure, imitate in cultivation.

It is a singular fact that cultivation has in some plants produced greater abundance of bloom and luxuriance of growth than they ever exhibit in their native haunts. This has especially been shown with some of the orchids of India and South America.

The fact is, to some extent, true of Rhododendrons; many species producing in our gardens larger and finer flowers than in their wild state.

In preparing for Rhododendrons, the situation of the bed is of primary importance. The plants will do well in any exposure, but they naturally love shade; and a northern hill-side is the best place for the bed. Our largest plantations are on a steep hill, sloping to the north-west, and exposed to the full fury of the winter storms. In such a situation not only do the hardy varieties do well, but even some kinds, considered tender in England, stand the winter uninjured.

In a southern exposure the foliage is seldom as fine as where the plants are sheltered from the full sun, though they sometimes set more bloom. A large bed on our lawn stood uninjured the parching summer of 1870, and is now in fine health, with a promise of abundant bloom for the coming year. The roots, however, never became dry, as the bed was kept moist by heavy mulching.

The test was, nevertheless, a very severe one, as
the bed was made by filling in an old gravel pit;
and the location was so hot and dry, that large
white pines, growing naturally close by, perished
from drought.

The fact that the Rhododendron thrives on a
northern exposure should of itself be a great incentive to its cultivation. What country place is there
which has not a bare northern slope, some cold
exposure where " nothing will grow " ?   Yet in
such a situation Rhododendrons will thrive ; change
it to a gorgeous mass of bloom in June, and give a
glorious show of rich evergreen foliage all the rest of
the year. Who will say the result is not worth the
necessary labor of preparation ?   And if we wish
flowers after the Rhododendrons, plant a few moun-
tain-laurel (*Kalmia latifolia*) for succession, and
here and there dot in bulbs of our noble American
lilies (*Lilium superbum* and *canadense*), with a few
clumps of the purple martagon, all of which bloom
magnificently ; and around the edges of the clumps
cultivate a host of the more dwarf-growing species
of our native plants which love a peat soil, such as
cypripediums, trilliums, and others, even to the
Christmas rose (*Helleborus niger*), to bloom often
to the dawn of New Year's morning.

We do not appreciate the wealth of our American
flora, and have shut our eyes to the richness which
lies around us.   In England, a crowning glory of
horticultural exhibitions is the show of " American
plants;" and we in America do not know what they
are.

The situation of the bed chosen, the first labor is excavation. If the surface is level, the soil should be removed to a depth of four feet, at least; if the soil is a dry gravel, another foot may be taken out advantageously.

Be the shape of the bed what it may, the soil should be picked out underneath the sides, as much as can be done without letting down the surface, in order that the soil around the sides may not be drained by the surrounding gravel. If the soil is a strong loam, and the subsoil clay, of such a nature that the water will not run off, loose stones to the depth of a few inches should be laid in the bottom of the bed, and a blind drain be laid to carry off surplus water : this, however, will rarely be necessary. The primary rule in Rhododendron culture is to *keep the bed always moist*, never very wet, never very dry ; for either extreme is injurious.

The bed excavated, fill in old litter, pine needles, leaves, or stubble, to the depth of two feet ; spread this, letting it lay loosely ; the soil, in filling, will press it down to a thickness of about six inches. This will keep the bed from draining too rapidly, and will in decaying furnish rich food for the roots, when in the course of years they reach it.

It must be borne in mind that the Rhododendron is not a deep-rooting plant,—the upper soil, if kept moist, will supply every need of the roots ; but it is to insure this moisture that so deep a bed is recommended.

In our own experience it has been necessary, for all our beds are dug out of loose gravel hills.

Where the soil is of a different nature such excavation may not be necessary, and in this each must be
his own judge.

There is some difference of opinion as to the best
compost for the beds. The component parts are
peat, loam, and sand: the proportions, however,
need not be exact.

Probably no two of our beds have been prepared
in exactly the same way, and yet in all the plants
have done perfectly well. As a general rule, we
have found a compost of five loads peat, five loads
loam, one load sharp sand, to be the best.

Where peat is not easily obtained, it will be sufficient to fill only the upper two feet of the bed with
the compost, the rest of the bed being good loam.

By peat we mean the dark, black soil, composed
of decayed vegetable matter, often fibrous, but never
hard. It should be dug out in summer, and spread
in thin piles for exposure to the action of the winter's
frost. In spring it will be of a loose and crumbling
texture, and ready for use. It should not be used
fresh, as it is then hard and sour: the more the frost
works upon it the better it is.

If it is difficult to find peat, meadow mud, leaf
mould from old woods, or any well-rotted vegetable
compost, may be substituted.

Our first Rhododendron bed was made wholly of
soil obtained from an old wood, where the mountain-
laurel (*Kalmia*) grew naturally, by scooping it out
from among the roots of the trees, and carting it
four miles.

The loam should be good garden soil, free from

stones. Old sods are a good filling for the lower part of a bed: care should be taken, however, not to use any containing couch grass, as the roots of this grass find the surface from a great depth, and are eradicated with great difficulty.

Any good clean sand, if free from stones and salt, is suitable: common building sand will answer every purpose.

Our mode of filling a bed is as follows: Three heaps of peat, loam, and sand, respectively, are made near the bed; two men, with long-handled shovels, fill from them, one throwing from the pile of peat, the other from the pile of loam, and in every eight or ten shovelfuls sprinkling in one of sand. The compost is thrown up against one side of the bed, which is raised to its full height, and the bed is thus gradually filled. Thus we have often planted one end of a bed before the other was filled.

This mode insures a thorough mixing of the component parts, and in beds thus made we have found the plants succeed much better than where the compost was mixed previously to filling.

Two of our largest beds are on a very steep hill facing the north-west, and their construction differs somewhat from the mode we have given.

The bed was first marked out on the surface as a large oval about midway down the hill, the object being to *look down* upon the plants when in bloom, which is always desirable if possible. The excavation was begun by digging out the soil to the depth of four feet along the upper side of the bed, and piling it along the lower side. This course was pursued, always pushing the soil out from the upper to the lower side, until an oval plateau was formed, just the size of the proposed bed, but everywhere four feet below the level of the upper line where the excavation was begun.

The whole bed was then filled in with soil prepared as we have described, four feet deep, so that a large level bed extended out at an angle to the hill-side. The heavy banks at the sides and lower part were then sodded, and the bed was ready for planting.

This is a most satisfactory mode of making a bed, and we should recommend it to every one who has a northern hill-side. It utilizes and beautifies a place where little else will grow, and the plants are more effective both in foliage and flower from their position. We should not advise such a treatment of a southerly slope, as the plants would probably suffer from the sun both in summer and winter.

PLANTING.

The bed being prepared, a few days should be allowed for the soil to settle to the level of the surrounding ground; then planting should begin. The time should be about the first of May in the latitude of Boston, but we have often varied it a fortnight earlier or later. If the plants have been imported, they will have come close packed in the cases, every interstice being filled with moss. In unpacking, the branches should all be carefully straightened out, and the plants, which always come with good balls of earth, placed in a covered, open shed, not exposed to the sun.

As soon as unpacked, they should be well watered overhead with a coarse-rosed water-pot, which will clean and freshen the foliage and moisten the balls. In this position they may be left for weeks without injury, moss being placed over the balls to prevent undue evaporation, and occasional waterings being given. It is, however, better to plant them within a few days after unpacking, if the weather is settled and favorable.

Plants obtained from nurseries in this country may be planted as soon as received.

There is nothing more simple than planting Rhododendrons. The plants have fine thread-like roots, which seize hold of and retain the soil; thus, unless very carelessly packed, they always come with good balls, and our only care is to place these balls in congenial soil.

A hole proportioned to the size of the ball should be dug in the prepared bed, the plant set as deep as it was before (or if a little deeper it will do no harm), the earth filled in and firmly pressed around the ball.

Waterings should not be given after planting: the balls having been well moistened after unpacking, the soil of the bed will be wet enough to keep the plants in good condition. Newly imported plants should be set rather close, so that the leaves almost touch, that during the first summer and winter they may protect each other.

All planting, however, must be done with an eye to the ultimate appearance of the bed. Thus, a bed

large enough for ten Rhododendrons of moderate
size may the first season contain a hundred. The
next spring, however, every other one should be
removed, and so on year after year.

In the first planting, care must be taken to so
arrange the plants which are to remain permanently,
that future transplanting may be avoided. This is
easily done by first setting them out in position, and
then filling in the others.

After planting, the surface of the bed should be
raked smooth, and prepared for

MULCHING.

We have said the Rhododendron is a surface-root-
ing plant, and therefore one great aim in cultivation
should be to keep the surface-soil moist. In old
beds, where the plants are masses of foliage, no ray
of sun will ever reach the ground, and the soil seldom becomes dry.

In new plantations we must prevent undue evaporation by mulching. The best mulch is spent tan,
which may be obtained at any tannery for a few
dollars a cord. It is cool and moist, the best pre-
ventive of evaporation, furnishes nutriment to the
roots as it decays, and accords in color so well with
the dark foliage of the plants as to produce a charming effect.

The tan should be spread evenly over the surface
of the bed from one to three inches deep, according
to the exposure of the bed to the sun. It should be
applied by the middle of May, before the surface has

had time to dry, and will not require renewal oftener than once in three years.

This mulching of tan seems particularly adapted to the plant: it is not infrequent for branches which chance to be bent down and covered with the tan to strike root; and we have many plants from such accidental layers.

Where tan cannot be procured, pine needles are the best mulch. These should be spread about two inches deep, and will last undecayed for years.

Oak leaves, or leaves of other deciduous trees, may be used where nothing better can be obtained; but they are objectionable, because they blow away, and give the bed and its surroundings a slovenly, ill-kept appearance.

Sawdust is too fine and close, preventing the access of air to the roots, which (as far as we can judge from our own experience), is of vital importance to Rhododendrons.

The coarse chippings from a boring machine would probably serve a good purpose if nothing better can be obtained. Meadow hay and litter are objectionable, as containing seeds of weeds and grasses, and forming a fermenting, decaying mass, injurious to the roots of the plants.

MANURING.

If the bed has been carefully prepared as we have directed, it will need no manuring.

Every thing of a stimulating, heating nature is injurious.

It is the best policy to do the work well at first, and then no further enriching of the soil will be needed. The roots of all "American Plants" feed on thoroughly decomposed vegetable matter. This we supply in abundance in the peat, of which the bed is composed, and as long as this nutriment lasts no more need be provided. It is, of course, within the range of possibility that in time, in old beds, this supply may be exhausted, and then a top dressing of peat, leaf mould, or even well-rotted stable manure, may be beneficially applied. Special manures, certainly any containing lime, would probably prove injurious.

Our own beds, some of which are ten years old, and contain plants twice that age, have never had a shovelful of manure of any kind, except what may have been derived from decaying tan, and are in vigorous health, growing stronger every year.

Where Rhododendrons are suffering for want of proper nutriment, the ground may be enriched; but all manure should be well rotted and thoroughly decomposed before application.

With liquid manures we have had no experience: we should, however, judge them to be of too stimulating a nature, and likely to prove injurious.

A mixture of charcoal with the soil is said to give intensity to the colors of the flowers. We see no reason to doubt the statement; but in view of the brilliancy of color in some of the varieties of recent origin, we see no need of such extraneous assistance.

PRUNING

May be performed freely when necessary. It was once thought that Rhododendrons could not bear pruning; but, on the contrary, they bear it remarkably well. We have had large plants, which were accidentally broken or cut down by the frost, produce young shoots as freely as rose-bushes, from wood an inch in diameter. As a fact, Rhododendrons need very little pruning: in growth they are symmetrical, and when left to themselves make such beautiful plants, that any attempts to prune them into formal shapes would prove wholly at variance with good taste.

Some tall-growing varieties, such as *R. Catawbiense album elegans*, need to be cut in when they grow too high. This may be freely done in early spring, or immediately after flowering.

We prefer, however, to rub out the terminal buds of shoots that would grow too high, just before the buds begin to swell in the spring.

When in bloom, Rhododendrons may be freely cut; the only care to be observed being to cut in such a way as not to injure the symmetry of the plant, or to leave bare places where there is no growing bud coming on to fill up the gap.

Standard plants occasionally need pruning; but, by a little care in rubbing out buds, the knife will seldom be needed for Rhododendrons.

TRANSPLANTING.

This is an easy process, and with a little care may always be successfully performed. We have said that the fine rootlets of the Rhododendron hold a mass of soil, so that the plants always "lift with a ball."

The only care is not to break the ball or to allow the rootlets to become dry. With these precautions Rhododendrons may be transplanted to any distance, and left out of the ground for a long time without danger of loss.

The season for transplanting is any time when the plant is not in growth. The Rhododendron makes its annual growth and ripens its wood in a few weeks in summer.

In most species, the growth is contemporaneous with, or closely succeeds, the flowering period; that is, with hardy kinds, from the middle of May to the middle of July, according to the species.

In a comparatively short time the growth is made, and the remainder of the summer the plants are forming the flowers or leaf-buds, and ripening the wood for the next year. By the middle of July we can usually tell how well the plants are to bloom the following June.

Some varieties often make a second growth; and, indeed, where the autumn is warm and moist, this is not an unfrequent occurrence. As this second growth seldom ripens well, and is usually killed by the winter, it should be prevented as much as possible. Plants in which this tendency exhibits itself should be planted in dryer soil, and kept quite dry during the months of August and September.

The only variety which we have known to ripen the second growth successfully is "Cunningham's Dwarf White" in its different kinds, the hardiest of the "*ponticum*" varieties, and which not unfrequently gives a pretty autumn bloom.

The best season for transplanting Rhododendrons is undoubtedly spring, say from the middle of April to the middle of May; but some cultivators move the plants in August, and there is no objection to autumn or winter transplanting, provided care is taken that the plants do not suffer by being thrown out of the ground by the frost.

A few years since, at one of the spring exhibitions of the Massachusetts Horticultural Society, there being a scarcity of pot-plants, we removed from the beds a number of large Rhododendrons in full bloom, some bearing hundreds of flowers, put them in large boxes, carted them into the exhibition, where they remained two days, and bringing them back placed them again in the positions whence they were taken. without the plants receiving the slightest check or injury. In England it is customary to bring hundreds of plants from great distances, just as they are coming into bloom, to form the celebrated exhibitions of American Plants yearly held in the cities, and to take them back again, the plants not feeling the removals.

Every autumn we take up hundreds of plants of the more tender kinds, some of immense size, set them in boxes, and keep them in cellars until spring, when they are replanted in the open air. The plants are not unfavorably affected, and bloom finely year after year.

Thus it will be seen that the Rhododendron, usually reputed a plant of difficult management, is capable of enduring quite as much hard usage in removal as any plant of our acquaintance; and this should serve as an additional incentive to its increased cultivation.

By a little attention to a reserve Rhododendron bed where a number of duplicates may be grown, we may yearly insure a display of bloom near the house, and produce gorgeous effects at will from masses of flowers.

TREATMENT AFTER FLOWERING.

As soon as the flowers have faded, the seed-capsules should be removed. This is a work of much labor, especially where the plants are large and tall. It must be done carefully, that the tender shoots, which are then just starting into growth at the base of the flower-truss, may not be broken or injured. The best way is to grasp the branch with the left hand close to the upper tuft of foliage, and with the thumb and finger of the right hand bend the truss of seed-pods to one side: it will usually break off clean, without injury to the young shoot.

The young wood coming from the base of a bloom-truss will not usually, except on very strong plants, set bloom the first year; but if the seed is removed, it may be depended on for strong bloom the following year. Thus we can easily regulate the bloom on any plant or portion of a plant, by removing bloom-buds one year to obtain a profusion of bloom the next.

Large and old plants, however, will always set as much bloom as they ought to carry; and the difficulty with Rhododendrons is rather overblooming than the contrary.

Some cultivators assert that the removal of the seed-vessels is not necessary. Yet they do not deny that ripening the seed weakens the plant for flowering; and the best reason given for neglecting it is that it takes too much time. We have tried both ways; and the superior beauty, vigor, and health of the plants from which the seeds were removed, has taught us always to do it at any expense of time and trouble.

Another objection to leaving the seed-vessels is that, when they have opened and scattered the seed, they become very hard and persistent, and are very unsightly, disfiguring the plant.

If the weather is very dry after the flowers have faded, the Rhododendrons should be plentifully watered. At this season they are in full growth, and need a great amount of moisture. This, however, should not be given after the young growth begins to harden; for then the object is to fully ripen the wood and mature the flower and foliage buds for winter. If the bed has been properly prepared, there will seldom be any need of watering; and mulching is always the best way of retaining moisture.

No weeds should be allowed to grow over the surface of the bed ; but *no spading* or *hoeing should ever be permitted.* The annual spading of shrubberies is a relic of barbarism, which should long ago have been discontinued in a civilized age.

DISEASES.

The Rhododendron has no diseases, at least this is in our experience; and of itself this fact should lead to its general cultivation.

INSECT ENEMIES.

These are very few, and seldom do any great injury.

We have occasionally noticed a branch in a dying condition, and upon investigation have found the pith eaten out by some species of borer; but have never been able to capture the insect in any state.

A species of saw fly sometimes cuts holes in the young foliage, but never to any great extent.

A year ago, noticing a young Rhododendron in bad health, and finding no apparent cause in the plant, we were led to examine the roots, upon which we found myriads of the white root aphis. This, however, is an exceptional case.

Our experience gives us the above facts, from which we deduce that insect enemies, as they exist at present, need deter none from cultivating Rhododendrons.

WINTER PROTECTION.

Rhododendrons vary much in hardiness. The greater part of the varieties found in English and continental catalogues are tender in the latitude of Boston.

Yet there are some magnificent varieties that are as hardy as a white pine, and which will endure uninjured our severest winters. But even these should be protected when first planted.

The first Rhododendron bed we ever made is on the north-western slope of a steep hill, exposed to the full force of the winter storms. It was planted ten years ago, with seven varieties of *Catawbiense* hybrids. For two years it was well protected in winter; but ever since it has stood without the slightest protection, entirely uninjured, although the mercury has at times fallen to fifteen degrees below zero. The plants are now ten feet high, immense masses of glorious foliage; and every June display thousands of gorgeous flowers.

Some of the more tender varieties endure the winter perfectly well if protected from the wind, and we may safely state that—of say seventy-five—of the hardiest of the *Catawbiense* kinds, the greater part will endure severe cold below zero, if they can be sheltered from the direct influence of the wind.

Even the hardiest kinds are sometimes injured in their foliage by the wind; and for this reason only we protect standards during the winter, as we shall fully describe in another chapter.

Evergreen boughs are the best winter protection for Rhododendrons. We use the common red cedar, it being of very dense growth, and plentiful in the neighborhood; but any evergreen will answer a good purpose.

The boughs of small trees are cut somewhat longer than the plants to be protected, and are stuck into the ground around the plant, in a slightly slanting position. When the ground freezes they become firmly fixed in position, and any weight of snow causes them to bend over and protect the plant. Thus it will be seen that this mode of protection is also useful in preventing the branches of young plants from being broken by the weight of the snow.

Another and an important object in protection is to keep the plants from the winter's sun.

Many reputed tender varieties are perfectly hardy if they can be kept in a frozen state all winter.

We can readily see that in our changeable climate, where the thermometer, at zero at sunrise, may by noon be fifty above zero in the sun, the evergreen leaves of plants are alternately frozen and thawed; and no doubt can be entertained that it is injurious to the foliage of the plants.

For this reason, Rhododendrons thrive better on a northern than on a southern exposure; and varieties, which on a bleak northern hill we never protect, on a lawn sloping to the south are carefully covered each winter.

While one great object of protection is to shelter the plant from wind and sun, any covering which deprives the plant of a free circulation of light and air is injurious.

Trussing up with straw, to us any thing but an attractive mode of winter protection, or covering with close boxes, are to be avoided.

Any protection, however, which will break the force of the wind, and partially shield from the rays of the sun, may be advantageously employed.

The time for covering Rhododendrons is just before the ground freezes up in the autumn, and the protection should be removed as soon as the frost leaves the ground in the spring. We generally cover the beds the last week in November, and remove the covering the first week in April.

In considering this question of winter protection, it must be borne in mind that our experience has been in the latitude of Boston, and near the sea coast.

Further south and in the interior, winter protection may be entirely dispensed with: in this matter experience is the best teacher.

Every year we are giving less protection as plants become acclimated and established; and ultimately may be able to dispense with it altogether for most varieties.

IMPORTING AND PROCURING PLANTS.

Although the Rhododendron is so well adapted for general planting, a large collection would be difficult to obtain in this country. The largest sale stock, to our knowledge, is that of Messrs. Parsons & Co., of Flushing, Long Island, who are now devoting a large portion of their extensive grounds to the raising of Rhododendrons.

In this collection are many fine specimen plants; and a good stock of young plants of such varieties as their experience has proved hardy and desirable, and of which we speak more fully in another chapter, are already for sale at reasonable prices. The plants in this nursery are grown in a deep, moist, rich loam, and such as have been supplied us have invariably done well. Messrs. Hovey & Co., near Boston, have many old and fine plants: their collection is grown in a natural meadow. They have also a fine stock of seedling *Rhododendron maximum*, the best species for massing on woody places and on rocky hills.

There may be other sale collections, but we have failed to find them. Every nurseryman's catalogue contains Rhododendrons, but probably not one in ten could supply half a dozen good plants. We have repeatedly ordered them, misled by an advertisement; and the result has been no plants, or, what was worse, a few ill-shaped, sickly specimens, only fit for the brush-heap.

The greater part of our plants have been imported from England, and yearly we thus add to our stock.

Probably the most extensive, as well as the oldest collection of American Plants, in England, is the Knap Hill Nursery, near Woking, Surrey, now of Mr. Anthony Waterer.

Thousands upon thousands of plants, in hundreds of varieties, are there annually grown for sale; and the nursery and grounds contain some of the largest and finest specimens in England. About the first of January we send an order to Mr. Waterer; and the plants leave England by steamer from the first to the middle of April, arriving in about a fortnight after shipping. They invariably come in good order, and we have never lost a plant from poor packing; nor have we ever had any occasion to complain of the quality of the plants. The cost of importing plants can easily be computed by reckoning an English shilling, cost price, at fifty cents currency. This is an outside figure, and includes gold, freight, exchange, and the outrageous imposition of a duty of thirty per cent in gold. By thus estimating, we can always be within our calculations.

American plants are extensively grown in most English nurseries, and catalogues before us contain large lists of varieties, and from any nursery plants could be imported. We, however, give the preference to Mr. Waterer, as his long experience enables him to send only such plants as are suited to our climate. Those who are in doubt what kinds to select can safely leave the choice to Mr. Waterer, and will be sure of receiving only the best plants.

STANDARD RHODODENDRONS.

These are amongst the most splendid ornaments of the garden, as those who have seen them in England will admit.

Some of our plants when in bloom are wonderfully beautiful, and are always attractive from the heads of rich glossy foliage.

Probably the largest standard in the country is on our lawn: the trunk is one foot one inch in circumference at the ground; it begins to branch four feet

from the ground, where it is eleven inches around;
it is eight feet four inches high, and the head is
twenty feet four inches in circumference; and the
whole plant requires in winter, to cover it, a shed
six feet square by nine feet high.

It is of the variety *roseum elegans*, which is particularly adapted for standards; and in June is so
covered with flowers as almost to conceal the foliage.

This plant was imported five years ago, and has
since stood uninjured two of the hardest winters
upon vegetation which we have known. We have
many other fine standards, both of hardy and tender
varieties: the former, with a slight protection from
wind and sun, are entirely uninjured by the winter;
the latter are removed to the Rhododendron cellars,
of which we give a description in a future chapter,
upon the approach of severe weather.

Our advice would be to all to plant a few standard
Rhododendrons. They are expensive; but one will
make more show than a dozen smaller plants, and
will not cost much more. In the centre of a bed, a
tall standard rising above the more dwarf plants is
especially effective.

The only care necessary is to be sure the plants
are worked on *Catawbiense* stock: those grown on
ponticum stock would be killed or injured by the
first winter.

In planting them, the position should not be too
sunny, as the hot suns of summer may injure the
tall trunks. We have sometimes, when the weather
was very hot and dry, pressed a large flower-pot into
the ground close to the stems of the standards, and

by filling it with water every morning a constant moisture was kept up from the slow percolation of the water through the hole in the bottom. These pots, however, are not ornamental, and are seldom necessary. Standards occasionally need pruning to keep the heads in shape; but a little attention to disbudding, as we have described, will render this unnecessary.

DWARF RHODODENDRONS.

These are among the most charming of the family, and no collection is complete without them. The greater part are perfectly hardy; and though in flower they are not so showy, yet in delicate beauty they far surpass the taller-growing varieties.

In this class we find the charming species *R. dauricum*, rather a loose grower, and needing severe pruning to make it symmetrical; but always beautiful in earliest spring, blooming with the crocus and outlasting the hyacinth.

Next is *R. Wilsonianum*, with beautiful glossy foliage, usually considered tender, but perfectly hardy with us; and then we have *R. odoratum*, the flowers of which, as the name implies, are delightfully fragrant.

R. hirsutum, and its variegated variety, are neat little plants, useful for the edges of beds, but are not particularly showy either in foliage or flower.

The charming Alpine *R. lapponicum* is most difficult of cultivation, but is beautiful enough to repay any care.

R. Torlonianum and *Govenianum,* both hybrids, are very pretty, but have with us proved rather tender.

R. punctatum can hardly be considered a dwarf. It is a pretty plant, but rather insignificant in flower.

R. ferrugineum is also rather tall-growing, and is showy in flower. This is the true " Alpen Rose."

We shall have more to say of all these in a future chapter, and only mention them in this connection to call special attention to their beauty.

CHAPTER II.

INDOOR CULTURE.

THERE are many of the finest species and varieties of Rhododendrons which are too tender to survive the winters of our climate. Many kinds, which in England are hardy, are tender with us, and can only be grown with indoor culture. In this class are all the fine varieties of *Rhododendron ponticum*, and many of those which have a mixture of *Catawbiense* blood; most of the best spotted and scarlet varieties, and many of those with the best-defined markings; all the glorious species of the Himalaya Mountains, the so-called " Sikkim Rhododendrons;" and all the various forms of the tree Rhododendron, *R. arboreum*, of Nepal; the yellow and buff-flowered Javanese species; and the delicate and beautiful kinds of which *Rhododendron jasminiflorum* is a representative.

Thus, we see that the indoor culture of this plant affords a far greater range than we can find in the garden. This culture has as yet, however, received but little attention: we find a few plants grown in greenhouses, but usually they are neglected and in bad condition. To grow Rhododendrons well, they should have a house to themselves; and with such culture the result would be the production of glorious masses of flowers during the early spring months. We know of no house of this kind, but one could be readily constructed at small expense.

It should be low, span-roofed; the sashes arranged to take off in summer, and shutters provided for covering the roof in early winter. The heating apparatus need not be very powerful, for the most that would be required would be to keep out the frost. The plants should be planted out in beds of prepared soil, and, by taking off the sashes, allowed to perfect their growth and mature their buds in the open air. When freezing weather approaches, the sashes should be replaced; and during the short days the house should be kept only a little above the freezing point. As the days lengthen, and the sun gains more power, more heat may be given, which will soon start the flower-buds.

According to the heat given, the plants will bloom from March to May, or by a selection of kinds a continuous bloom may be obtained. Such treatment would suit all the *ponticum* and the more tender *Catawbiense* hybrids: many of the Sikkim varieties would thrive and bloom, and some of the more tender species of other American plants might be added for variety. The tropical kinds, of course, require stove heat; but they are hardly numerous enough to warrant the erection of a special house.

Indoor culture is, in almost every respect, identical with garden culture, only it requires more care in watering, and air should be freely given on all occasions.

Such a house of plants in bloom would be a magnificent sight, and at other seasons it would require very little care.

FORCING.

Rhododendrons are very easily forced into bloom, and add greatly to the attractions of the green-house.

Any varieties may be forced, although a selection of the earlier blooming kinds would give those best adapted for the purpose. The plants for forcing should be selected in November from those best set with flower-buds: they should be carefully potted and removed to a cool, light cellar, where they should be kept until the first of January, receiving only sufficient water to keep the soil from drying up.

About the first of the year they should be gradually introduced into heat, and given a position near the glass. Water should be freely administered, but never allowed to stand around the roots. In a few weeks the buds will begin to swell, and the plants will rapidly come into bloom.

After flowering, the growth of the young shoots should be encouraged, keeping the plants as near the glass as possible to prevent them from becoming drawn. After all danger of frost has passed, the plants may be replanted in the bed from whence they were taken.

The same plants cannot be forced for two successive years, as they usually fail to set many flower-buds the second year; but a hundred plants will always supply plenty for annual forcing.

AS PARLOR PLANTS.

Many will be surprised at our recommending the
Rhododendron as a parlor plant; yet we know of
none more showy or of easier culture. We have
grown very fine specimens in a southerly window,
and had magnificent trusses of bloom during March
and April.

The process is very simple; being only to take up
the plants in autumn, pot them, and keep them in a
light, cool cellar, as above directed, and after the
turn of the year place them in the parlor-window.
The heat of furnaces or exhalations from gas-burn-
ers, which prove so fatal to most parlor plants, do
not seem to affect them, and they soon develop fine
trusses of bloom.

By a selection of varieties, fine contrasts of color
may be obtained; and, by taking some of the late
flowering kinds, a succession of flower may be main-
tained until the Rhododendrons bloom in the open air.

Parlor forcing is bad for the plants, as they seldom make good wood, the growth being generally
weak and long; but in a few years the plants re-
cover, and are again ready for forcing.

We have found " Cunningham's Dwarf White," in
its varieties, one of the best of the *ponticum* hybrids,
admirably adapted for parlor culture. We have also
successfully forced some of the most showy of the
Catawbiense hybrids, such as Nero, Lord John Russell, and Brayanum, with perfect success; and can
recommend parlor forcing to all lovers of Rhododendrons.

CHAPTER III.

PROPAGATION.

THE propagation of Rhododendrons is by no means difficult, although as yet it has been little attempted in this country. Old and approved varieties are increased by layers, cuttings, grafting, or inarching; and new varieties are obtained from seed.

These various processes differ in no degree in the case of this plant from the ordinary methods; but we will describe them briefly.

LAYERS.

By this means the best plants are raised, and it is the usual mode in England for propagating in large quantities approved varieties.

In its native swamps the Rhododendron roots readily wherever the branches bend to the ground, and become covered with soil or a débris of moist leaves.

In our own garden we have often obtained fine plants from branches which had by chance been covered by the earth of the bed or by the tan mulch, roots being very freely produced where the natural sufficiency of moisture is afforded.

We have only to bend the branch to the ground, to

2*

cover any portion of the old wood with the moist earth, and to secure the branch in position : roots will soon be protruded, and the second year the branch may be severed from the parent stock, to become an independent plant. The production of roots may be greatly facilitated by making an upward cut one half through the branch where it is to be buried deepest in the earth, in the ordinary manner of layering: the flow of sap is in a measure thus arrested.

These layers, if made in spring, will in two years be very strong, and ready to remove ; in some cases a single season may be sufficient for them, but ordinarily two years are required. The only attention necessary is to keep the branches in place by strong pegs, and the soil moist.

By layering the branches, tall, ungainly plants may be made in time fine specimens. The long, straggling branches should be bent down and firmly pegged at even distances all around the plant: they will root, and the bending of the branches between the old plant and the layers will facilitate the production of buds ; or, in gardener's parlance, the old wood will break, and the bare places be filled with new shoots, and the plant will become of a bushy, symmetrical shape.

CUTTINGS

Should be made of the half-ripened wood of the growing shoots. They should be inserted in silver sand, or peat and sand, and covered with a bell-glass.

No special attention is required, except to shade them from the direct sun, and to occasionally wipe the moisture from the glass: the sand, of course, should be kept moist. The cuttings root readily, and may then be transplanted to single pots, and the next season placed in the open ground.

Propagation by cuttings is seldom resorted to, except in the case of new varieties, and with the fine, tender species of the greenhouse and stove.

INARCHING.

This process is the same ordinarily employed for the propagation of camellias, and like hard-wooded shrubs.

Some vigorous stock of a common variety is selected. The branch should then be brought close to the stock, and the parts which fit best be carefully marked; next, at the places of contact, pare away the bark and wood for an inch or more in length on both stock and branch; then, letting the bark join exactly, tie the stock and branch tight together, and cover with clay or grafting wax. When the stock and graft are of the same size, a slit is made upward in the branch, and a corresponding slit downward in the stock; the parts are then tongued together, the whole joined exactly, tied, and covered with wax or clay as above.

If the operation is performed out of doors, both stock and graft should be carefully staked ; but in the house this is not necessary.

A few months will generally be sufficient to unite

the parts, and the grafts may then be separated from the parent plant.

They should be cut off close to the graft, and the head of the stock also removed. Inarching is sometimes called approach grafting, and is a very sure mode of propagation.

The best time for this operation is from January to April, or in summer: when performed in the house, the stocks should be well established in pots.

SEED.

By this mode innumerable varieties are raised, and thus all of the fine hybrids now in cultivation have been produced.

The seeds, which like those of most of the Ericaceæ, are small and fine, should be sown soon after ripening. They retain their vitality about a year; but the sooner they are sown the more certain is their germination.

The soil should be very fine peat and silver sand, in shallow boxes or pans: it should be made very fine and moist, the seed be thinly sprinkled on the surface, and just enough soil to cover it be sifted over the pan. The soil should be kept at a uniform rate of moisture, and be shaded from the direct rays of the sun and from frost. A close, cool frame is the best place. The time of germinating varies much with the season of planting, from a few weeks to six months. The seedlings are at first very small, and should be allowed to remain in the seed-pans until they attain some size. They should then be "pricked off" in pans or boxes, and grown in frames, with plenty of air in good weather, until large enough to be planted out.

In its native haunts the Rhododendron seeds very freely, and young plants are readily obtained.

In a recent journey through the Alleghany Mountains, we saw acres of Rhododendrons of the species *Catawbiense* and *maximum*. On one mountain side, where a stream ran along the road, myriads of plants had sprung up. They were of all sizes, from the tiniest plant to large trees; and we pulled up hundreds of nice well-rooted plants, which reached home in good condition.

In many places we found seedling Rhododendrons, Kalmias, and Epigæa rooting in the same cleft of the rock, and often so firmly it was impossible to dislodge them without destroying the plants.

HYBRIDIZATION

Has been but little attempted in this country. Some few good seedlings have been produced, but usually from chance seed.

The process is very simple, being only to fertilize a fine flower with the pollen of another, having previously removed the anthers of the female parent.

It is a good rule to make the hardier plant the female.

After fertilization, protect the fertilized flower by a gauze covering until it fades, and carefully gather the ripened seed.

Some of the seedlings recently produced in England are of wonderful beauty, combining depth and breadth of flower, brilliancy of color, and immense size of truss, with great vigor of constitution and beauty of foliage.

Of some of these we shall have occasion to give descriptions in future pages.

It is, however, very doubtful if any of them will prove thoroughly hardy, although in England they are the most splendid ornaments of the shrubbery.

Our aim should be to raise American seedlings suited to our climate.

Messrs. Parsons & Co. have a few, of which we think well so far as we have tried them. We also have exhibited for the last three years, at the weekly shows of the Massachusetts Horticultural Society, a well-marked seedling, which has proved very hardy. The color is very good, and the plant vigorous. These good qualities, with its hardiness, will probably render it valuable.

The field is wide and open to all; and what better can our nurserymen and amateurs compete in than raising hardy seedling Rhododendrons?

CHAPTER IV.

COMPARATIVE HARDINESS.

THE hardiness of Rhododendrons is a very difficult subject to treat.

Every cultivator will express a different opinion ;
and while on some few varieties all will agree, upon
the greater number no two will form the same opinion. The reason is simply that we are upon the
northern limit of hardiness for most kinds, and
the difference of a few degrees in the range of the
mercury is life or death to the plant.

Yet, strange as it may seem, some varieties, which
we find marked as tender in English catalogues, prove
hardy in the latitude of Boston.

An instance of this is the fine variety, " President
Van den Hecke," the flowers of which are blush
white, thickly spotted with chocolate, which has
with us stood the last three winters uninjured, both
in leaf and bud.

The hardest winters for Rhododendrons are those
when there is but little snow, when the mercury falls
below zero. The greater number of *Catawbiense*
varieties will stand uninjured where the thermometer
occasionally falls to zero ; but a long continuance
of zero weather is fatal to very many kinds. Snow
is a great protection : we repeatedly find plants

killed or badly injured above the snow-line, but bright and in good condition below.

Heavy falls of snow, however, sometimes do great damage by breaking the plants: we have had fine plants ruined by a thaw succeeding a heavy snow-storm, the snow settling and breaking all the branches, leaving only a tall stem with a few branches at the top. The covering of cedar-boughs is often a great protection against breaking by snow.

Of the hardiness of species we can speak with greater certainty.

All the Rhododendrons from Eastern and Central Asia, and the numerous "Sikkim" species, are tender. Some of the Himalaya kinds are precariously hardy in the south of England, and therefore might succeed south of Pennsylvania; but we do not suppose the experiment has been tried. A cold snap, such as that which has recently (December, 1870) visited the Southern States, would destroy them.

Rhododendron ponticum, and most of its varieties, are tender in New England: in the Middle States they would probably succeed. " Cunningham's Dwarf White," of which there are several varieties, (although a variety of *R. ponticum*), is hardy with us, some fifty plants having stood the last three winters uninjured, both in foliage and flower-bud.

This variety is said to be the only Rhododendron which will endure the winters of northern Europe.

Rhododendron hirsutum, punctatum, and *ferrugineum*, are hardy. *R. californicum* is not hardy in New England.

R. dauricum, and its variety, *atrovirens*, will stand in any exposure. *R. caucasicum* and *chrysanthemum* should prove hardy, but they are seldom found in cultivation.

R. lapponicum is a native of high mountain ranges and northern latitudes; but is an "Alpine" of difficult cultivation. In its native habitat it is probably protected by snow during the winter.

R. maximum is perfectly hardy; and any hybrids raised from it would probably partake of this characteristic.

R. Catawbiense is hardy as far north as Boston, though in severe winters the foliage has sometimes been a little browned.

The hybrids of *Catawbiense* vary greatly in hardiness. Though thus popularly called, they are of mixed blood, and are hardy just so far as they resemble the hardy parent. As a general rule, the bright colors and the deeply spotted varieties will be found tender; but we have great hopes that some of the newer seedlings, which in color are superior to any of the old kinds, may prove hardy with us.

In the description of varieties in Part II., we propose to give our experience of the hardiness of the several kinds. We must say, however, that the experience of one locality is not necessarily that of another, differing but little in climate. Each one must experiment for himself with doubtful kinds, and thus only can he ascertain the true rule for his guidance.

There are many Rhododendrons that in branch and bud are hardy, but of which the foliage is dis-

figured every winter. The result is, the plants look
badly the greater part of the year, and the flowers
are small and poor. These varieties should be discarded. A great beauty of the Rhododendron is the
foliage; and as a variety which keeps its foliage
unhurt occupies no more room, and requires less care
than one which is thus partially tender, the hardy
varieties should be preferred. Greater attention is
now being paid in the production of seedlings to size
and color of foliage, and some of the new kinds are
of surpassing excellence in this respect.

HOUSES FOR WINTER PROTECTION.

Standard Rhododendrons, even of the hardiest
kinds, are liable to have the foliage very much disfigured by the cutting winds of winter. It is difficult
to protect or screen very large plants with cedar-
boughs; therefore we must protect them otherwise.

We have found rough houses, made of light boards,
to answer this purpose perfectly.

Those we use vary greatly with the size of the
plant: some are so small one man can place them;
others so large it takes half a dozen men to put them
in position.

They are not ornamental, but could easily be
made so, though this would increase their weight.
The matter of appearance is of little importance, as
they are in use only from the middle of December
to the first of April. In their construction we must
bear in mind that they are not to protect against
cold, but only against direct wind; so we must not

make them tight. Those we use are made with a sloping roof, the joints battened to keep rain from leaking on to the plant; the sides of light boards, nailed about an eighth of an inch apart, to allow a free circulation of air. The northerly side is in one piece, and is secured by screws: in the middle of this side is a square window, a foot or more wide, which is covered with a piece of white cotton-cloth. The house is moved on from the southerly side, then the northerly side is screwed on, and the plant is housed for the winter. With this protection, the standards come out in the spring with fresh foliage and in splendid condition.

When not in use, the houses are stored in some remote shed.

GROUPING

Is of great importance for effective display. The different species and varieties differ greatly in habit and foliage. Some are only suitable for the front of the bed; others look well only in the background. Color of flower also enters as an element in planting for effective display.

While experience in this must be, in a measure, the teacher, some hints may be given which may prove advantageous.

Thus, of two fine white-flowered varieties, both excellent and equally hardy, *album elegans* is a tall-grower, and only suited for the middle or rear of a bed; and *coriaceum* is very dwarf, and in any position but the front would be lost.

In Part II. we shall give the habit of the variety where it is peculiar, in order to aid the planter.

Rhododendrons are particularly adapted for specimens, and never look better than when so planted. Large masses are, however, very effective in foliage, and of wonderful magnificence when in flower. In their native habitats the plants grow in huge masses, and any one who has seen a Southern " Laurel swamp" in bloom will never forget its beauty. Some of the hills of the Alleghany Mountains present masses of Rhododendrons, than which one cannot find a finer sight in the floral kingdom. We can, in cultivation, excel nature in variety, if not in quantity. We have masses of Rhododendrons which, when in bloom, are sheets of color, — white, pink, scarlet, and purple; and no more beautiful sight can be imagined.

In planting masses, regard need not be had to keeping the plants separate. Give each room to develop, and then let the branches mingle : the effect is far more natural and beautiful. Varieties should also be arranged as to color to present the best contrasts when in bloom : this is easily done by selecting named kinds. Those which bloom at the same season should be planted together: there is a difference of many weeks in the flowering of species and varieties.

Thus, *Rhododendron dauricum* blooms with the crocuses ; but *R. hirsutum* not until the middle of June. *R. grandiflorum* is with us a week earlier than any of the *Catawbiense* hybrids ; while *R. Hannibal* is the latest of all, seldom blooming until all the others have faded. *R. maximum* does not bloom until after the first of July.

Those kinds which bloom very early or very late should be planted as specimens, or in masses by themselves; thus a continuous and effective bloom may be obtained.

In the new seedlings, many are late bloomers; and this is a great gain, as thus the Rhododendron season is prolonged.

In grouping, some attention should be paid to foliage: the flower lasts only a few weeks, the foliage the whole year; therefore those varieties with greatest breadth of foliage, of a bright or very dark green, should be chosen for the front of the bed.

PART II.

DESCRIPTION OF THE RHODODENDRON.

PART II.

DESCRIPTION OF THE RHODODENDRON.

RHODODENDRON PONTICUM.

THIS species has been longest in cultivation, and there are in England many very large plants. It does not grow very tall, the largest of which we have any record being about fifteen feet high ; but it spreads its branches over a large space, and is not unfrequently found thirty feet in diameter. Many of the large plantations in England are of this species, and it is extensively planted for game covers, as the buds are not eaten by rabbits. Seedlings are very easily raised, and are furnished by nurserymen for about twenty shillings per hundred for flowering plants a foot high. It grows freely in any good loam, and flowers abundantly.

The flowers are purplish, and, though in the mass very showy, are wanting in substance. The foliage, though good, is by no means so handsome as in many other species.

This species is a native of Armenia, the Levant, Georgia, the Caucasus, and various parts of Asia extending to the Himalaya Mountains.

It is not hardy in New England, and probably would not succeed well north of Philadelphia: although it would doubtless survive with a slight protection, or even unprotected in ordinary winters, south of New York. Where it is hardy, its cheapness, and the facility with which it adapts itself to different soils, render it a most desirable plant for massing on hill-sides and in open woods. Figured in Bot. Mag. 18, t. 650.

There are many hybrid varieties and named seedlings, some hardier than the species and very well worth growing. Of these we may especially mention: —

R. P. FOL. ARGENTEIS, FOL. AUREIS, FOL. MARGINATIS,

The kinds with silver and gold striped foliage which are desirable, as the markings are distinct and permanent. The plants grow freely, and are ornamental. The flowers are poor. Our plants are wintered in a cold cellar, and planted out in summer.

VARIETY CUNNINGHAM'S DWARF WHITE.

This is the hardiest of the pontic varieties, and has with us stood the winter perfectly well for the last four years.

The foliage is more glossy, and brighter, than in the species; and the flowers vary from pink to pure white.

It is a rapid grower, though of dwarf habit; and flowers very freely. For forcing there is nothing better, as even in a parlor window it will bloom in a few weeks after being brought from the cellar.

Plants may be imported for about fifty cents each.

We heartily recommend this variety for general planting.

Variety ALBUM. This is merely a white-flowered variety of the species, and is only desirable for planting with it for contrast.

Variety SALICIFOLIUM and CHEIRANTHIFOLIUM, the willow and wall-flower leaved, are very pretty for contrast, the foliage being narrow and somewhat curled. The flowers are small; pale purple. Our plants do well wintered in the cellar.

Variety AZALEOIDES is a hybrid with some species of azalea. The leaves are small, and the flower not especially showy; the plant is dwarf, and suitable for the borders of beds. With us it has stood eight winters, flowering freely; but the leaves are liable to be browned by the winter's sun without protection.

A sub-variety, *crispiflorum*, figured in Illus. Hort. 5, t. 181, has very showy flowers; rich pink, with wavy petals.

Variety PICTUM is very distinct, and worthy a place in the choicest collection; color white, with very dark spots on upper petals; requires cellar protection in winter.

Found in catalogues as *Lowii*.

Variety MULTIMACULATUM is a very neat variety; flowers white, spotted with red; tender.

Variety NIVATICUM is a very fine flower ; white, spotted with pale yellow; tender.

Variety BLANDUM, a good pale blush kind ; tender.

Variety ROSEUM has rosy flowers, not especially desirable with so many better flowers of the color ; tender.

Variety AUCUBÆFOLIUM is a very distinct kind, with spotted leaves. The flowers are light lilac, and very pretty. It has stood the winter with us for three years uninjured.

Variety TORTULOSUM has light green and curiously contorted foliage. It is only desirable as a curiosity.

Variety FLORE PLENO is desirable if any one wishes a double-flowered Rhododendron. The color is pale purple, the flower of good form ; but it is wanting in the simplicity and beauty of the single varieties.

It seems tolerably hardy, having stood the last four winters with us in a northern exposure, the flower-buds surviving, and the foliage only being slightly browned one year.

Variety HYACINTHIFLORUM is another double-flowered kind, and open to the same objection as the last-mentioned. The flowers are very double ; and the plant is a good grower, and blooms freely.

It has proved hardy with us.

Variety VERVANEANUM is also double-flowered. We cannot speak as to its hardiness.

Variety GUTTATUM is delicate and pretty. The flowers are white, distinctly spotted. Well worth growing, but tender.

There are other varieties, varying in color from deep purple to pure white, some very pretty and desirable, and all worth planting for experiment.

It is impossible to tell whether these will prove hardy, and the only course is for each cultivator to try them for himself. As the plants are very cheap, the experiment cannot prove expensive.

We have given descriptions of those which we have grown at Glen Ridge, and probably any which we have found hardy will prove so anywhere south of the latitude of Boston. We do not, however, advise the amateur who only plants a few Rhododendrons to choose any of the pontic varieties. They are less showy than others, and may be cut off at any time by a winter of unusual severity.

RHODODENDRON MAXIMUM.

This is the Rose Bay, or Great Laurel, of the New England States ; and is found plentifully from southern New England southward. The farthest northern limit is a swamp near Sebago Lake, near Portland, Me.; it next occurs in a large swamp on the banks of Charles River, in Medfield, Mass., and next in a swamp in Randolph, south of the Blue Hill.

In Medfield it was till recently very abundant, and flowered so freely that we have seen wagon loads of flowers gathered; but the tall trees which sheltered it have been cut down, and the plants in many places chopped off even with the ground. So a few years hence, it may be extinct in that locality.

The plant is a tall grower, of loose habit ; foliage large, dark green above, rusty or whitish beneath. The flowers are small, white or pinkish, with yellowish-green spots on the upper petals.

This species is the latest blooming Rhododendron we have, never blooming until after the first of July, in New England.

It is common in cultivation, the plants having been brought from the swamps ; and plants are often seen for sale at the large markets, in the spring. It is, however, the least desirable of all the Rhododendrons, its only merit being its late flowering. For large masses on the banks of ponds or on shady hill-sides, it is to be recommended, as it is perfectly hardy. It will not bear drought, however, as well as other species, and does not do well in full sunshine. The only losses of Rhododendrons from the excessive drought of the past summer (1870), at Glen Ridge, have been large plants of *Rhododendron maximum*. Figured in Bot. Mag. 24, t. 951; in Michaux, vol. 3, pl. 4 ; and in Big. Med. pl. 51.

In English magazines we find mentioned as varieties *maximum album, purpureum,* and *Wellsianum*. The first is probably little different from the species, and is the *R. Purshii* of Loudon. The second is

the *R. purpureum* of Pursh, which never existed as
a species, is not now recognized, and is probably
some hybrid of *R. Catawbiense*. Of the last we have
been able to obtain no information. It is said by a
writer in the " Cottage Gardener " to have " pink
flowers, fine foliage, and to be of good habit; " if so,
it must be indeed desirable.

RHODODENDRON DAURICUM.

This charming species we place among the most
desirable of Rhododendrons, not so much for the
beauty of the individual flowers as for its hardiness,
its early blooming, and the abundance of blossoms.
It is a native of Siberia and Eastern Asia. The
foliage is deciduous; the flowers are rosy-purple, and
appear in very early spring before the leaves. A
mass of this plant is a charming object in early
spring; and no collection, however small, should be
without it.

Figured in And. Rep. 1, 4; Lodd. Cab. 605 and
1446. Bot. Mag. 17, t. 636.

Variety ATROVIRENS is also a native of Siberia, and
differs only from the species in having dark evergreen leaves, which render it more desirable, as when
in bloom it is more effective.

Figured in Bot. Mag. 44, t. 1888; and in Lodd.
Cab. t. 1584, under the name of *sempervirens*.

These plants naturally grow tall and spindling,
and are much benefited by careful pruning.

They may be imported for about fifty cents a
plant.

RHODODENDRON CALIFORNICUM.

This species is a native of California, and is well
worthy of cultivation wherever it proves hardy.
The chances are, it will not stand the winters in
New England.   In England it is hardy, a writer
in the "Cottage Gardener" calling it the "hardiest
Rhododendron" he has "met with, standing wind
well."

The flowers are rosy, very showy; and the habit
of the plant is good.   Figured in Bot. Mag. 81,
t. 4863.

RHODODENDRON ARBOREUM.

A noble species, native of Nepal, attaining larger
size than any of the family, the trunks being found
twenty feet high and twenty-four inches in diameter.
The foliage is large, dark green above, silvery beneath ; the flowers bright scarlet, in dense heads.

This species varies much in the color of the
flowers : in the wild state they are found of every
shade, from deep scarlet to pure white ; and in cultivation numerous varieties have been raised, differing
greatly in color, markings, and size of flowers, and
in foliage.

Some of these are among the most valuable Rhododendrons for greenhouse culture and for forcing.
With us all are tender, and require greenhouse
protection.   As they bloom very early in the spring,
they are not suitable for outdoor culture, even if
protected by removal to the cellar in winter.   For

a tender Rhododendron house they are perfectly adapted, and furnish a variety of brilliant colors not to be found in other species.

The species is figured in Bot. Reg. 11, t. 890; Hook, Ex. Fl. t. 168; Pax. Mag. 1, p. 101, and 2, p. 98; Sweet's, Fl. G. 250.

The following are native varieties: —

Variety ALBUM has white flowers, with delicate purple spots. Figured in Bot. Mag. 61, t. 3290; and Bot. Reg. 20, t. 1684.

Variety ROSEUM has bright rosy flowers. In its native country this variety is higher up the mountains than the scarlet species, and is hardier. Figured in Bot. Reg. 15, t. 1240; and in Sweet's Fl. G. t. 339.

Variety NIVEUM is a charming variety, with white flowers, spotted with purple. Figured in Sweet's, Fl. G. t. 148.

Variety CINNAMOMEUM has rosy-white flowers, spotted with brown. The foliage is rusty on the under side. A very showy plant. Figured in Bot. Mag. 67, t. 3825.

The figure in Bot. Reg. 23, t. 1982, under this name, is a different plant.

Variety PAXTONI is a fine kind, with deep crimson flowers of great substance. Figured in Pax. Mag. 14, p. 99.

This variety should not be confounded with the *Catawbiense* hybrid of the same name.

The following are hybrid varieties : —

Variety RUSSELLIANUM is a hybrid between *Cataw-biense* and *arboreum*; color, bright crimson. Figured in Sweet's, Fl. G. 2, t. 91.

Variety SMITHII COCCINEA has scarlet flowers, beautifully spotted; a hybrid between *R. ponticum* and *arboreum*. Figured in Sweet's Fl. G. 2, t. 50.

Variety ALTA-CLARENSE was raised from *R. arboreum*, fertilized with a seedling between *ponticum* and *Catawbiense*. The flower is clear, bright, transparent scarlet, and the foliage very rich. Figured in Bot. Reg. 17, t. 1414; and in Bot. Mag. 62, t. 3423.

Variety UNDULATUM is a hybrid with *R. ponticum*. The flowers are deep, shaded purple; and the foliage has a peculiar, wavy form. Figured in Sweet's Fl. G. t. 341.

Variety ALBUM SPECIOSUM, figured in Illus. Hort. 1, t. 1, has white flowers, beautifully spotted with crimson.

There are many other fine hybrids, and new ones are constantly produced. All are showy in flower ; but many popular this year will be lost a few years hence, giving place to varieties of newer origin. Some of the old varieties we have mentioned still hold their place as standard kinds, and are as yet unsurpassed.

The tendency now is to raise hardy Rhododendrons ; but the tender kinds should not be neglected, as they comprise some of the most beautiful of the family.

Many other hybrids, in which the blood of *R. arboreum* is mingled, are mentioned in future pages. Indeed, it is to this species we owe much of the high coloring found in some of the most popular varieties.

RHODODENDRON ALBIFLORUM.

A very distinct and beautiful species, native of high regions in the Rocky Mountains. It is a low shrub, bearing the leaves in tufts at the ends of the branches, and below them a few small drooping creamy-white flowers, which bear little resemblance to those of other Rhododendrons. It first bloomed in England in 1837, but probably is not now in cultivation. Figured in Bot. Mag. t. 3670, and in Hook. Fl. Bor. Am., vol. 2, p. 43, t. 133.

RHODODENDRON ANTHOPOGON

Is a small-flowered species, with rusty leaves and yellowish-white flowers, not especially ornamental. It is not hardy. A native of the Himalayas. Figured in Bot. Mag. 68, t. 3947.

RHODODENDRON CAMPANULATUM.

This is a magnificent species, native of the mountain of Gosainthan, in Nepal. In England it is hardy, but the flowers expand so early as to be often injured by the frost; therefore, with us it would require house protection. The flowers are rosy-lavender, with dark spots; the foliage deep green, rusty underneath. Figured in Bot. Mag. 66, t. 3759; and in Sweet's, Fl. G. II. t. 241.

The variety *R. c. superbum* (Pax. Mag. 16, p. 190) has waxy white flowers, spotted with crimson-purple.

RHODODENDRON CAUCASICUM.

This is a small species, in its native country forming a low shrub, with procumbent branches; a native of the Caucasus, on high rocks, near the limits of perpetual snow.

The flowers are white, tinged with purple or rose.

It is a desirable species, and should prove hardy with slight protection. Figured in Bot. Mag. 28, t. 1145.

Variety STRAMINEUM has straw-colored flowers, and is a very handsome plant. Figured in Bot. Mag. 62, t. 3422.

Variety ALBUM is a hybrid with the white variety of *Azalea pontica*, and resembles an Azalea more than a Rhododendron. Figured in Bot. Mag. 67 t. 3811.

Variety PULCHERRIMUM is a hybrid between *arboreum* and *caucasicum*. The flowers are rosy, and very showy.

Variety NOBLEANUM has bright scarlet flowers, and is a very beautiful kind. There are also sub-varieties with rose and pink flowers; but that called *Nobleanum superbum* is the best.

RHODODENDRON CHRYSANTHUM.

This pretty little species is a native of Siberia and other extreme northern countries: it is also found in the Caucasus Mountains. It is a low shrub, never exceeding one foot in height, with evergreen leaves, and large, irregular, yellow flowers.

While perfectly hardy, it is difficult to cultivate, the heat of summer probably affecting it unfavorably. It is rarely found in cultivation. Figured in Wood. Med. 2, 103; and in Steph. Med. 2, 80.

RHODODENDRON PUNCTATUM.

This pretty species, although a native of Carolina and Georgia, generally stands the winter with us; although the foliage is usually somewhat disfigured, and the flower-buds are killed if the mercury falls much below zero. The foliage is dark green, covered below with rusty dots, whence the name; the flowers are small, pink, very pretty, but not especially showy. The habit of the plant is straggling. It is worth growing in a collection, but is only interesting for variety. Seedlings vary much in shade and markings of the flowers.

Figured in Bot. Mag. 49, t. 2285; Bot. Reg. 1, t. 37; and And. Rep. 1, t. 36.

Sometimes called *R. minus*.

RHODODENDRON HIRSUTUM.

A low-growing species, and the most common of the dwarf Rhododendrons. The leaves are small, evergreen, thickly covered with rusty hairs; the flowers pale red, in small clusters.

Native of the Alps, and one of the flowers most commonly sent home in collections of Alpine plants. This and *R. ferrugineum* are known as the " Alpen Rose."

This plant is useful for the edges of beds of American plants, but is not showy. Figured in Bot. Mag. 43, t. 1853.

Variety VARIEGATUM is a more showy plant than the species, and the foliage variegated with yellow is very pretty. It can be readily obtained from England, but is not common.

RHODODENDRON FERRUGINEUM.

Although this plant and the last are considered by some botanists as but varieties of one species, the differences are quite sufficient to abundantly distinguish them. The foliage of *R. ferrugineum* is smooth above, rusty and dotted below, and far larger than *R. hirsutum;* the flowers are also much larger, lighter-colored, and the habit of the plant is taller. The buds seldom open until other Rhododendrons, except *R. maximum*, are out of bloom; and this renders it a very valuable species.

The blossoms cover the whole plant, and, though not brilliant in color, in the mass are very showy. It stands the coldest winters uninjured, will grow in any moist garden soil, and never fails to bloom.

Figured in Lodd. Cab. t. 65, though the flower is too bright in color.

Variety ALBUM, figured in Sweet's, Fl. G. II. t. 258, has white flowers. We do not now find it in any catalogues.

RHODODENDRON LAPPONICUM.

A small Alpine species, growing about six inches high, with small violet-purple flowers. We have not seen it in cultivation, although it can easily be obtained from the White Mountains. Probably, like all Alpines, it would prove of difficult cultivation.

Figured in Bot. Mag. 58, t. 3106.

RHODODENDRON KAMTSCHATICUM.

A low-growing species, with purple flowers, native of Kamtschatka; probably not now to be found in cultivation.

RHODODENDRON CHAMÆCISTUS.

This species, in foliage, is wholly unlike a Rhododendron, the leaves rather resembling some species of thyme. It is a native of the European Alps and of Siberia; and would probably prove hardy, with slight protection, such as a winter covering of pine-needles, as it never exceeds a few inches in height.

The flowers are large, for the plant; pale purple, and very handsome.

Figured in Pax. Mag. 3, p. 169; Bot. Mag. 14, t. 488; Lodd. Cab. 1491.

We now come to the most showy of the family, the magnificent species of the Sikkim Himalayas. Of these we can only briefly cite from English authorities. We have had no experience in their culture. They are all tender, — many true green-house plants; others will stand a few degrees of frost. These latter are worthy of cultivation in a Rhodo-dendron-house.

The magnificent work of Hooker, on the " Rho-dodendrons of the Sikkim Himalaya," from which we derive most of our information, gives beautiful colored figures of these noble species. We have also given references to such figures as we have been able to find in other illustrated works; but our notice of all these species must necessarily be brief, and can only serve to call the attention of the amateur to the wealth of floral beauty which is within his reach.

All the best species can now be obtained of Eng-lish nurserymen, and many fine hybrids have been originated within the last ten years.

We also mention some of the tropical Rhododen-drons: species of easy growth with stove-heat, many of which are exquisitely beautiful, and some deliciously fragrant.

RHODODENDRON DALHOUSIÆ.

This species, one of the noblest of the family, produces flowers three to four inches in diameter ; white, tinged with rose, and very fragrant.

It is parasitical on the trunks of oaks and magnolias, in its native habitat ; but in cultivation does not require the treatment of an epiphyte, growing freely in the ground or inarched on other species. No description can do justice to its beauty ; but some idea may be formed by reference to the illustrations in Hook. Rhod. tab. 1 and 2 ; Bot. Mag. 79, t. 4718, and 88, t. 5322 ; Fl. des Serres, 5, t. 460–468.

RHODODENDRON BARBATUM.

A tall-growing species, attaining the height of sixty feet ; the leaf-stalks covered with long bristles, or hairs. The flowers are blood-color, in a close, compact head : very handsome. This species has proved hardy in England. Figured in Hook. Rhod. pl. 3 ; and Fl. des Serres, 5, t. 469–472.

RHODODENDRON LANCIFOLIUM.

A shrubby species, with lanceolate, coriaceous leaves, and small, close heads of rich crimson flowers ; nearly allied to the foregoing, but wholly destitute of hairs.

Figured in Hook. Rhod. pl. 4.

RHODODENDRON WALLICHII.

A shrub attaining a height of about eight feet, with showy foliage, and large lilac flowers, with rosy dots. In foliage this species is distinct from all others.

Figured in Hook. Rhod. pl. 5. It is, however, regarded as a form of *R. campanulatum*, and as such is figured in Bot. Mag. 82, t. 4928.

RHODODENDRON CAMPBELLIÆ.

A species often attaining the height of forty feet, and only distinguished slightly, botanically, from *R. arboreum*. Flowers scarlet, in close heads.

Figured in Hook. Rhod. pl. 6.

RHODODENDRON ROYLII.

A low-growing shrub, with brownish-red flowers, tipped with blue; not a very showy species.

Figured in Hook. Rhod. pl. 7.

RHODODENDRON CINNABARINUM.

A small species, very distinct both in foliage and flower; the former beautifully reticulated, the latter of a fine cinnabar color.

Figured in Hook. Rhod. pl. 8.

Variety PALLIDUM has fine rose-colored flowers, in an irregular terminal umbel. Figured in Bot. Mag. 80, t. 4788.

RHODODENDRON ELÆAGNOIDES.

A little known, low-growing species, from the snowy regions of the Himalayas. The flowers are usually yellow, but vary to deep-red purple.

Figured in Hook. Rhod. pl. 23.

RHODODENDRON ARGENTEUM.

A tall-growing, magnificent species, with leaves a foot long, by three or four inches in breadth. Flowers white, two or three inches long, and as much in diameter.

Figured in Hook. Rhod. pl. 9; Bot. Mag. 84, t. 5054; and Fl. des Serres, 5, t. 473–476.

RHODODENDRON FALCONERI.

A large tree, with immense leaves, downy on the under side; and heads of numerous, small, white flowers. A very distinct and striking species.

Figured in Bot. Mag. 82, t. 4924; Fl. des Serres 5, t. 477, 480, and 11, t. 1166–67; Hook. Rhod. pl. 10.

RHODODENDRON VACCINIOIDES.

A very small, straggling, epiphytal species, much resembling in growth and appearance the Himalaya vaccinum (*V. obovatum*). The flowers are unknown.

Rhododendron niveum.

A species much resembling *R. arboreum*, but distinguished by the snow-white under surface of the foliage. Flowers light lavender-white color.

Figured in Lem. Jar. t. 421 ; and Bot. Mag. 79, t. 4730.

Rhododendron obovatum.

A small, resinous shrub, with small red flowers ; nearly allied to *R. lepidotum*.

Rhododendron lepidotum.

A species with small flowers, existing in two varieties ; the one with yellow, the other with reddish-purple flowers.

It is a pretty species. Although native of high mountains, it would probably prove tender.

Figured in Lem. Jar. pl. 343 ; Bot. Mag. 78, t. 4657, and 80, t. 4802.

Rhododendron Aucklandii.

A magnificent species, the flowers often measuring five inches in diameter. Color white, tinged with pink. Leaves four to ten inches long, bright green.

Figured in Revue Hort. 1855, 5 ; Hook. Rhod. pl. 11.

This plant is sometimes referred to *R. Griffithianum*, as a variety. See Bot. Mag. 84, t. 5065.

RHODODENDRON THOMSONI.

A shrubby species, noticeable for the deep blood-red color of the flowers, and their glossy surface. Foliage roundish.

Figured in Fl. des Serres, 7, t. 688–690; Hook. Rhod. pl. 12; Bot. Mag. 83, t. 4997; Revue Hort. 1855, t. 7.

RHODODENDRON PENDULUM.

An epiphytal species, native of damp, gloomy forests, on the branches of pine-trees. Shoots long, straggling; leaves dull green, rusty below; flowers small, white. Figured in Fl. des Serres, 7, t. 662; and Hook. Rhod. pl. 13.

RHODODENDRON PUMILUM.

This is the smallest of the Sikkim Rhododendrons, and one of the rarest and most beautiful. Leaves about half an inch long; flowers very delicate rose-color.

Figured in Fl. des Serres, 7, t. 667; and Hook. Rhod. pl. 14.

RHODODENDRON HODGSONI.

A common Himalaya species, forming immense masses of jungle. Foliage large; deep, brilliant green. Flowers in close heads, pale purple or rose-color.

Figured in Revue Hort. 1855, 22; Hook. Rhod. pl. 15; Bot. Mag. 92, t. 5552.

RHODODENDRON LANATUM.

A small tree-like species; leaves yellowish-green, tawny white below. Flower pale sulphur-colored, with red dots. A very pretty plant.

Figured in Fl. des Serres, 7, t. 684; and in Hook. Rhod. pl. 16.

RHODODENDRON GLAUCUM.

A pretty little plant, with glaucous foliage and pale purplish-pink flowers.

Figured in Bot. Mag. 79, t. 4721; Revue Hort. 1855, t. 11; Hook. Rhod. pl. 17; Fl. des Serres, 7, t. 672.

RHODODENDRON MADDENI.

A magnificent plant, with large, campanulate, white flowers, often tinged with pink. Foliage clear green, tawny below.

Figured in Bot. Mag. 80, t. 4805; Fl. des Serres, 9, t. 912; Hook. Rhod. 18; Revue Hort. 1855, 16; Illus. Hort. 1857, t. 140.

RHODODENDRON TRIFLORUM.

A small shrub, with pale greenish-yellow flowers much resembling an azalea, growing in clusters of three.

Figured in Fl. des Serres, 7, t. 673; Hook. Rhod. pl. 19.

RHODODENDRON SETOSUM.

A small-growing species, much resembling a Rhodora in habit and flower. Leaves box-like, and evergreen; flowers purplish, freely produced. The whole plant is strongly and disagreeably resinous. A native of the highest mountains, and very showy when in bloom. It would probably be hardy.

Figured in Hook. Rhod. pl. 20.

RHODODENDRON EDGEWORTHI.

An epiphytal species, with superb flowers and neat, small foliage. Flowers white, tinged with blush or pale yellow, often four inches in diameter.

Figured in Fl. des Serres, 8, t. 797–8; Hook. Rhod. pl. 21; Bot. Mag. 82, t. 4936.

RHODODENDRON ÆRUGINOSUM.

A shrubby species, native of altitudes 15,000 feet above the level of the sea. Flowers lilac-rose, in small, close heads.

Figured in Hook. Rhod. pl. 22.

RHODODENDRON SALIGNEUM.

A slender plant, with pale glaucous-green, drooping leaves. Flower light yellow, spotted with green, about an inch in diameter. A pretty species.

Figured in Hook. Rhod. pl. 23.

RHODODENDRON CILIATUM.

A small shrub, attaining the height of two feet; the whole plant hairy. Leaves dark green. Flower pale reddish-purple, very pretty. This species is one of the most easily grown of the Sikkim kinds, and flowers freely.

Figured in Pax. Fl. G. t. 83 ; and Hook. Rhod. pl. 24.

Variety ROSEO ALBUM differs in having rosy-white flowers, and, like the species, blooms freely when only a few inches high. This was the first of the Sikkim species which flowered in cultivation.

Figured in Lem. Jar. t. 312 ; Bot. Mag. 78, t. 4648 : Fl. des Serres, 8, t. 766.

RHODODENDRON FULGENS.

A native of high latitudes, and a very showy plant. Flowers in round, close heads, of a deep, glowing scarlet color. Foliage roundish; tawny below.

Figured in Bot. Mag. 88, t. 5317 ; Fl. des Serres, 8, t. 789 ; Hook. Rhod. pl. 25.

RHODODENDRON NIVALE.

A little plant, growing only two inches high, and attaining " a loftier elevation than any other shrub in the world." It much resembles *R. lapponicum*. The foliage is very small; the flower about one-third of an inch in diameter, purple.   The whole plant has an odor resembling cologne.

Figured in Hook. Rhod. pl. 26.

RHODODENDRON VIRGATUM.

A very slender, twiggy species, from Bootan. Flowers reddish-purple, solitary or in pairs.   Foliage very glaucous.

Figured in Hook. Rhod. pl. 26.

See also Bot. Mag. 84, t. 5060; and Fl. des Serres, 14, t. 1408, for varieties which differ, in having pink and white flowers, and in their disposition, — which is in the one axillary, in the other terminal.

RHODODENDRON WIGHTII.

A very large tree, with showy foliage; rusty cinnamon-color below, rich green on the upper surface.   Flowers bell-shaped, in dense clusters; yellow, beautifully marked with red.   A splendid species.

Figured in Fl. des Serres, 8, t. 792-3; Hook. Rhod. pl. 27.

RHODODENDRON CAMELLIÆFLORUM.

A singular epiphytal species, found growing upon pine-trees.   Stems slender; foliage small; flowers white, resembling a single camellia.

Figured in Hook. Rhod. pl. 28; and Bot. Mag. 82, t. 4932.

4

RHODODENDRON CANDELABRUM.

This plant, of which a beautiful figure is given in Hook. Rhod. pl. 29, is considered by Dr. Hooker as a pale-flowered variety of *R. Thomsoni.* (Hook. Rhod. pl. 12.) There are, however, some slight botanical differences between the two.

RHODODENDRON CAMPYLOCARPUM.

This species is a small shrub, and is one of the most charming of the Sikkim Rhododendrons. Foliage bright green ; flowers bell-shaped, sulphur-yellow, spotless, and fragrant.

Figured in Hook. Rhod. pl. 30 ; Bot. Mag. 83, t. 4968.

RHODODENDRON NILAGIRICUM.

This plant much resembles *R. arboreum,* of which it may prove a variety. By some, however, it is considered identical with *R. Campbelliæ.* It is a native of Nepal, and bears large trusses of rosy-pink and white flowers.

Figured in Fl. des Serres, 10, t. 1030–1 ; and Bot. Mag. 74, t. 4381.

RHODODENDRON FORMOSUM

Is a native of Silhet, in the east Himalaya range. The flowers are large, white, fragrant, and very showy.

Figured in Bot. Mag. 75, t. 4457.

RHODODENDRON GIBSONI

Is a very fine species, with large, white flowers, with yellowish shading. The young foliage resembles an azalea.

Figured in Pax. Mag. 8, p. 217; and Fl. des Serres, 1, t. 18.

RHODODENDRON JAVANICUM.

This is a tropical species, but will thrive and bloom freely in a warm greenhouse. The foliage is bright glossy green; the flowers orange-yellow, but very variable in shade.

Figured in Bot. Mag. 73, t. 4336; Pax. Mag. 15, p. 217; Fl. des Serres, 3, t. 293-4.

Variety AURANTIACUM (Fl. des Serres, 6, t. 576) has trusses of vivid orange flowers, lighted with rosy tints.

RHODODENDRON CITRINUM.

This small species is also a native of Java. The flowers are small, drooping, light yellow.

Figured in Bot. Mag. 80, t. 4797; and in Fl. des Serres, 10, t. 970.

RHODODENDRON JASMINIFLORUM.

This elegant species is a native of Malacca. The flowers are tubular, white, with deep pink eye; the foliage neat and showy. From this species some beautiful hybrids have been produced.

Figured in Lem. Jar. t. 41; Bot. Mag. 76, t. 4524; Illus. Hort. 1859, t. 203.

RHODODENDRON CHAMPIONÆ.

This beautiful species is a native of Hong Kong. Botanically, it is nearly allied to *R. formosum*. The foliage is distinctly veined; the flowers rosy, or reddish-pink, shading to a white throat, with broad, spreading petals.

A variety is described with delicate, white flowers, the upper lip pale yellow, towards the centre copiously dotted with ochre.

Figured in Lem. Jar. t. 208; and Bot. Mag. 77, t. 4609.

RHODODENDRON FARRERÆ,

Figured in Sweet's Fl. G. 2, t. 93, is a small, pink-flowered species from China. The flowers are very pretty, resembling azaleas. Probably not in cultivation.

RHODODENDRON METTERNICHI.

This is a Japanese species, a native of high mountains, and would doubtless prove hardy. The flowers are rather small, rosy-white, something like those of *R. maximum*.

Figured in Sieb. Fl. Jap. pl. 9.

RHODODENDRON ALBUM.

A very pretty Javanese species, with whitish-yellow flowers; foliage dark green, rich rust-color below.

In habit this species resembles *R. citrinum*. A stove plant.

Figured in Bot. Mag. 83, t. 4972.

RHODODENDRON BATEMANI

Resembles as a species *R. campanulatum*. Flowers large, deep crimson-red. Native of Himalaya.

Figured in Bot. Mag. 89, t. 5387.

RHODODENDRON BLANDFORDIANUM.

A Himalayan species, very variable both in flower and foliage. Color brick-red, orange, or even greenish.

A fine figure is given in Illus. Hort. 3, t. 112. See also Bot. Mag. 82, t. 4930; and Fl. des Serres, 11, t. 1173.

RHODODENDRON BOOTHII.

A very showy, tender species, from Central Asia. Flowers small, bright yellow; foliage, when young, very hairy. Figured in Illus. Hort. 3, t. 174.

RHODODENDRON BROOKIANUM.

A rare and splendid kind, native of Borneo, and, in its wild state, epiphytal. Flowers large, rich golden yellow.

Figured in Bot. Mag. 82, t. 4935; and Fl. des Serres, 12, t. 1238–9.

RHODODENDRON CALOPHYLLUM.

A fine species, native of the Bootan Mountains, where Mr. Booth discovered sixteen new species, emulating the example of Hooker, who found forty-three in the Sikkim Himalayas.

Flowers large, white, very showy.

Figured in Bot. Mag. 83, t. 5002; also in Hen. Ill. Bou. pl. 19.

RHODODENDRON GRANDE.

A tall-growing species from India. Figured in Wight, vol. 4, t. 1202.

Probably not in cultivation.

RHODODENDRON GRIFFITHIANUM.

A fine species, with large, white flowers. Figured in Wight, vol. 4, t. 1203. *R. Aucklandii* (Bot. Mag. 84, t. 5065) is sometimes referred to this species.

RHODODENDRON HOOKERI.

One of the Bootan species, of tall habit, and only found at high elevations. Flowers very regular, of rich scarlet color.

Figured in Bot. Mag. 82, t. 4926.

RHODODENDRON KENDRICKII.

A species with dark foliage, which varies much in width. Flowers in large trusses, scarlet.

Figured in (variety *latifolium*) Bot. Mag. 85, t. 5129.

RHODODENDRON KEYSII.

A very singular species, wholly dissimilar in flower from all other Rhododendrons. The flowers are dull red, tipped with pale yellow, and are produced in clusters from the old wood. In habit it is a small shrub, a native of Bootan, and has proved hardy in England.

Figured in Bot. Mag. 81, t. 4875; and Fl. des Serres, 11, t. 1110.

RHODODENDRON MOULMAYNENSE.

A small, slender-growing species, producing delicate white flowers, tinged with yellow. Native of Moulmain.

Figured in Bot. Mag. 82, t. 4904.

Rhododendron Shepherdii.

One of the Bootan kinds, much resembling *R. Kendrickii.* Flowers deep scarlet, in large trusses. Figured in Bot. Mag. 85, t. 5125.

Rhododendron Nuttallii.

A superb species; in Bhotan, its native country, forming a tree thirty feet high. The leaves are nearly a foot long, and the single, white flowers measure six inches in diameter. It is not a free bloomer in cultivation. The flowers are white, shaded to light yellow, and are very beautiful.

Figured in Bot. Mag. 85, t. 5146; Fl. des Serres, 13, t. 1326; Illus. Hort. 1859, t. 208; Hen. Ill. Bou. pl. 21.

Rhododendron Retusum.

A native of western Java and Sumatra, generally on high mountains. The flowers are small, but of a bright scarlet color, very rich and showy; foliage bright evergreen.

A fine figure of this plant is given in Illus. Hort. 2, t. 76. See also Bot. Mag. 81, t. 4859; Fl. des Serres, 10, t. 1044.

Rhododendron Smithii.

Another of the Bootan species. Foliage rich dark green; flowers rich red, in large, close heads. Figured in Bot. Mag. 85, t. 5120.

RHODODENDRON VEICHIANUM.

A magnificent species, from Moulmain. Flowers very large and showy, white, with wavy petals, as in some of the Indian azaleas.

Figured in Bot. Mag. 83, t. 4992 ; Fl. des Serres, 14, t. 1416, and 15, t. 1519–20.

RHODODENDRON WINDSORII.

A Bootan species, which proves hardy in England. Foliage dull, opaque green ; silvery below. Flowers rosy-red or white.

Figured in Bot. Mag. 83, t. 5008.

RHODODENDRON LOBBIANUM.

A fine stove species, from Penang, intermediate between *R. javanicum* and *Brookianum*. Foliage bright evergreen ; flowers bright yellow.

Figured in Fl. Mag. pl. 10.

RHODODENDRON THIBAUDIENSE.

This pretty species is nearly related to *R. Keysii*, which it resembles in the peculiar form of the flowers ; but, unlike that species, they are terminal, and not produced on the old wood. It is a very showy plant, native of Bhotan.

Figured in Fl. Mag. pl. 253.

4*

RHODODENDRON FORTUNI.

A Chinese species, resembling — both in foliage, form of flower, and fragrance — *R. Griffithianum ;* but differing in color of flower, which is in this plant a delicate rose. Hardy in England.

Figured in Bot. Mag. 92, t. 5596.

It is not improbable that the next few years may give us new species of these magnificent Rhododendrons. The mountains of Asia have proved wonderfully rich in new plants, and seem the true kingdom of this glorious flower. The beauty of the species already known is such that it seems impossible that finer kinds can be discovered. We have already beauty, size, and richness of foliage; color, size, symmetry, and fragrance of flower; and good habit in the plant, — which leave us nothing to expect and nothing to desire.

The varieties we now mention are hybrids, generally from species we have already described.

RHODODENDRON APRILIS.

A hybrid between *ponticum* and *dauricum ;* color rose. Figured in Bot. Reg. 29, t. 62.

Probably lost from cultivation.

RHODODENDRON ALSTROMERIOIDES

Is a cross between an azalea and *R. caucasicum album.* The flowers are prettily spotted, but there are hundreds of better kinds.

Figured in Lem. Jar. t. 384.

RHODODENDRON WILSONI,

Figured in Bot. Mag. 85, t. 5116, is a hybrid between *R. ciliatum* and *R. glaucum*. The flowers are rosy-red, and very pretty.

RHODODENDRON PRECOX.

An early-blooming variety, raised from *R. dauricum atrovirens* and *ciliatum*. The flowers are bright rosy-lilac, and freely produced. Probably hardy.

Figured in Fl. Mag. pl. 58.

RHODODENDRON PRINCE OF WALES (Rollinson's)

Is a hybrid between *R. javanicum* and *retusum*. Flowers tubular, orange, very showy. Requires stove culture.

Figured in Fl. Mag. pl. 155.

RHODODENDRON CARNEUM.

Flowers pale pinkish-white, with green spots; a hybrid between *R. arboreum* and some variety of *Azalea sinensis*.

Figured in Fl. des Serres, 1846, t. 3.

RHODODENDRON CARTONI,

A seedling between *Azalea nudiflora* and *Rhododendron Catawbiense*, has pretty purplish flowers, with lighter centre, much resembling *R. Govenianum*. The foliage is evergreen in ordinary winters.

Figured in Bot. Reg. 17, t. 1449.

RHODODENDRON CAUCASICUM ARBOREUM

Is a hybrid between *R. arboreum* and *caucasicum*. The flowers are pink, and very pretty. Figured in Maud. Bot. 4, p. 157.

R. venustum of Sweet, Fl. G. 2, t. 285, is the same plant.

RHODODENDRON DENISONI

Was raised from *R. Dalhousiæ*, crossed with *R. Edgeworthi* and *Gibsoni*. The flowers are large, white, lighted with straw-color.

Figured in Fl. Mag. p. 291.

RHODODENDRON ALBUM SPECIOSUM.

A tender, white - flowered variety, beautifully spotted.

Figured in Illus. Hort. 1, t. 1.

RHODODENDRON SESTERIANUM.

A cross between *R. Edgeworthi* and *Gibsoni*. Flowers white, very large, marked with reddish-yellow spots.

Figured in Illus. Hort. 9, t. 345.

RHODODENDRON PRINCESS ALEXANDRA,

A hybrid from *R. jasminiflorum*, has large, fragrant, white flowers, tinged with pink.

Figured in Fl. Mag. pl. 245.

RHODODENDRON PRINCESS HELENA

Was also raised from *R. jasminiflorum*, fertilized with a scarlet seedling. The flowers are long, tubular, bright pink, and very showy.

Figured in Fl. Mag. pl. 220.

RHODODENDRON PRINCESS ALICE

Is the result of crossing *R. ciliatum* and *Edgeworthi*. The flowers are very large, pure white, the buds tipped with pink.

Figured in Fl. Mag. pl. 206.

RHODODENDRON MADAME VAN HOUTTE

Is a hybrid of *R. maximum*, and of course hardy. The truss is very large, the flowers bright pinkish-white.

Figured in Fl. des Serres, 15, t. 1606–7.

RHODODENDRON OTHELLO (Van Houtte)

Is also a hybrid from *R. maximum*, which it resembles in the shape of the truss. Flowers deep reddish-purple.

Figured in Fl. des Serres, 12, t. 1274.

RHODODENDRON GRAND DUC DE BADE

Is derived from the hybrid *omnigutlatum*, fertilized with *R. cinnamomeum*. The flowers are white. flaked all over with dark reddish-purple.

Figured in Illus. Hort. 11, t. 423.

RHODODENDRON MADAME WAGNER

Is a hybrid from *R. caucasicum*. The flowers are white, edged with cherry, the petals crimped.
Figured in Illus. Hort. 2, t. 66.

RHODODENDRON MADAME PICOULINE

Is a hybrid between *R. ferrugineum* and *arboreum*. The flowers are white, intensely spotted.
Figured in Illus. Hort. 3, t. 84.

RHODODENDRON OMNIGUTTATUM

Is probably derived from *R. ponticum*. Flower small bright rose, beautifully marked with crimson.
Figured in Illus. Hort. 7, t. 244.

RHODODENDRON MYRTIFOLIUM

Is a cross between *R. hirsutum* and *punctatum;* a hardy variety, suitable for small beds, or the edges of larger ones. Flowers reddish-pink.
Figured in Lodd. Cab. t. 908.

RHODODENDRON FRAGRANS.

This is a chance seedling from *R. Catawbiense,* probably hybridized with an azalea. The foliage is fine evergreen; the flowers pale purple, and fragrant. A desirable hardy variety.
Figured in Pax. Mag. 10, p. 147.

RHODODENDRON HYBRIDUM

Is a dwarf, neat variety, of uncertain parentage. While very pretty, the foliage has with us been badly cut up by the winter. The plant figured under this name in Bot. Reg., t. 195, is not that now known as such.

RHODODENDRON GOVENIANUM.

This variety was produced from a hardy azalea, crossed with a hybrid of *R. ponticum* and *Cataw-biense*. With us it is not an evergreen, except in very mild winters. Flowers fragrant, pale reddish-purple; habit slender, much resembling an azalea.
Figured in Sweet, Fl. G. 1, t. 263.

RHODODENDRON TORLONIANUM.

A hybrid, like the last, and in habit much resembling it.
The flowers are whitish purplish-pink, but vary in shade. Both this and the last variety suffer somewhat in severe winters; and, while pretty, they are not especially to be recommended.

RHODODENDRON ARBOREUM CINNAMOMEUM

Was raised from seed obtained by crossing *R. maximum* with *R. cinnamomeum*. The foliage is very large, and tawny below; the truss large; flowers white, with dark purple spots.
Figured in Pax. Fl. G. p. 16.

RHODODENDRON COMTESSE FERDINAND VISANT.

A seedling of Van Houtte's, from *R. campanulatum*, fertilized with *R. cinnamomeum*. Flowers creamy white, bordered with delicate rose.

Figured in Fl. des Serres, 9, t. 935.

RHODODENDRON DAPHNOIDES.

This is a pretty dwarf variety, of which we have been unable to find the origin. The flowers are pink or rose-colored, and very pretty.

RHODODENDRON OVATUM.

Another dwarf variety, with rosy flowers and neat foliage. Both this and the last are generally hardy, although the foliage often gets browned by the winter.

RHODODENDRON COUNTESS OF HADDINGTON.

A hybrid, between *R. Dalhousiæ* and *ciliatum;* of neat, evergreen habit, and large, white, blush-tinted flowers. Figured in Hen. Illus. Bou. pl. 82.

RHODODENDRON AUREUM MAGNIFICUM.

This variety, which is probably the same as that figured in Sweet, and which we have before mentioned under the name of *R. Smithii aureum*, is one of a lot of seedlings produced by crossing a Rhododendron with a species of yellow azalea (*A. sinensis*). In habit they are robust; the foliage is sub-evergreen, partaking of the character of both parents.

The following list we copy from "Henderson's Illustrated Bouquet," where a fine plate is given : —

Aureum magnificum. . . clear bright yellow; large truss.

„ *punctatum* . . primrose, spotted with orange.

„ *superbum* . . fine yellow, deep orange spots.

Album flavum . . . . blush white, orange-yellow spots.

Bianca . . . . . pure white, yellow spots.

Burlingtonii . . . . bright yellow; large truss.

Carneum versicolor . . yellow - pink edging, finely spotted.

Congestum aureum . . good yellow; compact truss.

Cupreum . . . . . rich coppery - orange, suffused with pink.

Delicatum aureum . . blush pink, with large blotch of orange spots.

Gloriosum . . . . . white, spotted with yellow.

Jenkinsii . . . . . lemon, tinged with pink; large truss.

Macranthum flavum . . shaded pink, with buff-yellow centre.

Ornatum . . . . . sulphur - yellow, with orange spots ; large truss.

Primulinum formosum . clear primrose - yellow, orange spots.

„ *elegans* . . light primrose, with pale spots ; compact truss.

We are not aware that any of these have been tested in this country, but hope soon to be able to report from experience upon their merits and hardiness.

RHODODENDRON CATAWBIENSE.

Magnificent as are the flowers of the Himalayan and Bhotan Rhododendrons, it is not too much to say that our gardens owe more to this species than to any other. A large proportion of the species and varieties we have described are tender or precariously hardy. But for the garden and shrubbery we need plants which will endure any winter, and for these we must look to the so-called " *Catawbiense* hybrids."

The species is a native of the Southern States, usually upon the mountains. It is a tall shrub, with lilac-purple flowers, evergreen foliage, and quite a pretty species; but the parent is seldom grown, being lost in the multitude of seedling varieties. To trace the parentage of these varieties is generally impossible. They range in color from rose or white to deep purple, and vary greatly in foliage.

Every year hundreds of thousands of seedlings are raised, the best of which receive names, and are thrown upon the market: most of these, in turn, give place to newer, yet often no better kinds, although from the first there has been a steady improvement in color, constitution, and foliage.

In the following list we have selected those which the popular verdict in England has pronounced the best. A large number of them are in our own collection; and we describe them as hardy or tender, according to our experience.

Where figures of any have been given in illustrated periodicals, we have referred to the plate. For convenience we give the list alphabetically.

Many of these have the blood of many species; and some, perchance, have no trace of *Catawbiense*, yet, as hardy garden Rhododendrons, their place seems to be in this list, and, without vouching for parentage, we call the class

CATAWBIENSE HYBRIDS.

ACHIEVEMENT . . . One of Anthony Waterer's new seedlings of 1870; rosy-scarlet, with a clear white centre; very showy.

ACLANDIANUM . . . Delicate blush, deeply spotted with chocolate; precariously hardy.

ACUTILOBUM . . . . Cherry-red, shaded; truss large, petals acute. Figured in Illus. Hort. 4, t. 149.

ADMIRATION . . . . Bright rosy-crimson, very dark spots.

ALARIC . . . . . . Dark purple, shaded with crimson or plum color; large truss and flower; hardy.

ALARM . . . . . . A very beautiful flower; centre white, edged with pale scarlet or crimson; flower rather small; tender.

ALBUM . . . . . . Pure white; free bloomer, fine foliage; hardy.

ALBUM ELEGANS . . Blush, changing to white; large flower, tall habit, good foliage; perfectly hardy.

ALBUM GRANDIFLORUM Flower like the last, but somewhat larger; truss large; fine foliage; perfectly hardy.

ALBUM TRIUMPHANS . A very fine white, large flower.

ALEXANDER ADIE . . Brilliant rosy-scarlet; close, handsome truss.

AMILCAR . . . . Bright violet-purple, with a reddish tinge, intense blotch of black spots on the upper petal. Figured in Fl. Mag. pl. 18.

AMBROISE . . . . . White, bordered with rich cochineal-red; tender. Figured in Fl. des Ser. 8, t. 945.

ANDERSONI . . . . White; good foliage; hardy.

ANGE VERVAET . . Clear pink, white throat, intensely spotted with carmine. Figured in Fl. des Ser. 18, 1870–1.

ANNIHILATOR . . . Bright rosy-scarlet.

ARCHEDUC ÉTIENNE . White; upper petals deeply spotted with maroon-brown. Figured in Illus. Hort. 13, t. 491.

ARCHIMEDES . . . . Bright rosy-crimson, with lighter centre; very distinct; hardy.

ASCOT BRILLIANT . . A seedling of John Standish, from *R. Blandyanum* with *R. Thomsoni*: flowers deepest blood-color, having the appearance of being crystallized.

ATHENE. . . . . . White, with yellow blotch.

ATROSANGUINEUM . . Deep blood-red; flower of great substance, fine foliage; hardy.

ATTILA . . . . . . Dark purple, shaded with crimson; hardy.

AUGUSTUS . . . . . Same as ALARIC.

AUGUSTE VAN GEERT. Light rosy-purple, marked with brown.

AURORA . . . . . Bright rosy-lake; free and late bloomer.

AZUREUM . . . . . Bluish-lilac; hardy.

BARCLAYANUM . . . Deep rosy-crimson; fine truss and foliage; late bloomer; hardy.

BARON CUVIER . . . Lilac, chocolate blotch.

BARONESSE LIONEL } White, with scarlet-crimson
ROTHSCHILD . . . } margin.

BERTIE PARSONS . . A seedling of Parsons & Co., of Flushing, Long Island; of good form, and lilac-pink or mauve color, with brown eye; hardy.

BICOLOR . . . . . Rose, clear white spot on the upper petals; hardy.

BIJOU DE GAND . . White, edged with rose, beautifully spotted; tender. Figured in Illus. Hort. 7, t. 261.

BLANCHE SUPERBE . . Waxy white, green eye.

BLANDYANUM . . . . Deep rosy-crimson; beautiful flower; fine habit and foliage; hardy.

BLATTEUM . . . . . Claret-crimson, shaded and spotted; fine form and truss; precariously hardy.

BRABANTIA . . . . Dark rich crimson.

BRAYANUM. . . . . Vivid crimson, lighter centre;
fine foliage and truss; a
dazzling flower; generally
hardy.

BRENNUS . . . . . Rich crimson-lake.

BRILLIANT. . . . . Crimson-scarlet; free bloomer,
dwarf habit; same as SUN OF
AUSTERLITZ; tender.

BROUGHTONI . . . Rosy - crimson; fine foliage;
large truss; tender.

BRUTUS . . . . . . Pale rose, large flower.

BYLSIANUM . . . . Clear white ground, the tips of
the petals edged with bright
crimson-pink; a very beautiful variety. Figured in Illus.
Hort. 5, t. 155; and Hen.
Illus. Bou. pl. 18.

CANDIDISSIMUM . . . Blush, changing to pure white;
tender.

CANDIDISSIMUM (Par-
sons') . .   . . . Pure white; hardy.

CANDIDUM .   . . . Blush.

CARACTACUS . . . . Rich purplish - crimson; fine
truss ; foliage and habit;
probably hardy.

CHANCELLOR . . . . Light purple, deeply spotted;
large truss ; hardy.

CHARLES BAGLEY . . Cherry - red; fine truss; probably hardy.

CHARLES DICKENS . . Dark scarlet; fine foliage; a
beautiful variety; probably
hardy.

CHIONOIDES . . . . Creamy white, fine form.

CLIMAX . . . . . . Deep scarlet-crimson, with dark spots on the upper petals; probably hardy. Figured in Fl. Mag. pl. 65.

CHLOE . . . . . . Crimson-lake, spotted.

CLIVEANUM . . . . Pinkish - white; large truss; tender. Figured in Bot. Mag. 75, t. 4478.

CLOWESIANUM . . . White, purple spots. Figured in Fl. des Ser. 13, t. 1315.

CŒLESTINUM . . . . ⎫ Blush, yellow eye.
CŒLESTINUM PICTUM . ⎬ Blush, purple-spotted.
CŒLESTINUM GRANDI- ⎪ Blush, yellow eye; large truss,
FLORUM . . . . . ⎭ and fine foliage; all fine, hardy varieties.

CŒRULESCENS . . . Bluish white; hardy.

COLUMBUS . . . . . Clear purple, spotted; hardy.

CONCESSUM . . . . Light centre, clear rosy-pink margin; an exquisite variety; tender.

CONGESTUM ROSEUM . Light rose, dark spots; fine foliage.

COMET . . . . . . Bright scarlet.

COMTE DE GOMER . . White, edged with rosy-crimson; fine form. Figured in Illus. Hort. t. 230.

CORIACEUM . . . . Yellowish, changing to pure white; dwarf, free blooming; hardy.

CORREGGIO . . . . Clear dark scarlet.

COUNTESS OF DEVON . French white, rosy edges; upper petals spotted with purplish-crimson. Figured in Fl. Mag. pl. 162.

CRUENTUM . . . . . Rich lake, fine deep color; probably tender

CURRIEANUM . . . . Dark rosy-lilac, spotted; fine form and truss; precariously hardy.

DECORATOR . . . . Clear bright rose, dark spots.

DELICATISSIMUM . . . Blush-white, tinted with pink; hardy.

DESDEMONA . . . . Blush, richly marked on the upper petals.

DONA MARIA . . . White, tinged with pink, deeply marked with yellow and red spots. Figured in Fl. des Ser. 10, t. 1040.

DORKINSII . . . . . Dark, clear chocolate-crimson.

DUC DE BRABANT . . Salmon-white, spotted; semi-double; tender.

DUCHESS DE NASSAU . Pink, white centre, intensely spotted with brown. Figured in Illus. Hort. 12, t. 450.

DUCHESS OF SUTHER- ⎫ White centre, shading to broad
LAND . . . . . . ⎭ margin of rosy-lilac.

DUKE OF CAMBRIDGE . Bright crimson-scarlet, pale centre.

DUKE OF NORFOLK . Clear rose; same as RUBENS.

E. C. BARING . . . Glowing crimson; fine habit; a new seedling of Anthony Waterer.

EDWARD S. RAND . . Another of Mr. Waterer's new seedlings; crimson; immense truss; fine *Catawbiense* habit; probably hardy.

ELFRIDA . . . . . Bright rosy-crimson, dark spots: a fine flower.

EMINENT . . . . . Rosy-lilac.

ERECTUM . . . . . Rosy-crimson; good habit.

ÉTENDARD DE FLANDRES Lavender-white, finely spotted; generally hardy. Figured in Fl. des Ser. 8, t. 783–4.

ÉTOILE DE VILLIERS . Rose, shading to white, deeply marked with yellow spots. Figured in Fl. des Ser. 11, t. 1084.

EVERESTIANUM . . . Rosy-lilac, spotted and fringed; fine foliage; free bloomer; the best hardy Rhododendron.

FASTUOSUM FLORE PLENO . . . . . Lilac, fading to lavender; immense truss of double flowers, remaining long in bloom; very showy and desirable; precariously hardy. Figured in Fl. des Ser. 2, t. 143–4.

FAUST . . . . . . Pale lilac, beautifully blotched.

FLEUR DE FLANDRES . Reddish-pink, deeply spotted with purple and green. Figured in Fl. des Ser. 17, t. 1816–17.

FLEUR DE MARIE . . Bright rosy-crimson, blotched with white.

FRANCIS DICKSON . . Brilliant scarlet; a fine late bloomer; probably tender.

GEMMIFERUM . . . . Rosy-crimson, light centre.

GENERAL CABRERA . Crimson, with blotch of dark spots; large flower; tender.

GENSERIC . . . . . Purplish-crimson, shaded to scarlet.

GEORGIANUM . . . . Light pink, distinct.

GIGANTEUM . . . . Light rose; large truss; fine foliage; hardy.

5

GLENNYANUM	Light pink ; pretty, but tender.
GLORIOSUM	Blush-white; large flower; hardy.
GRANDIFLORUM . . .	Clear rose; fine truss; good foliage; free bloomer; and very hardy.
GLOIRE DE BELLEVUE	Rose, finely spotted.
GUIDO	Crimson; probably hardy.
GULNARE	Blush-pink ; fine form.
HANNIBAL	Rose, shading to blush and lighted with white ; a fine, late-blooming, hardy kind.
HENDERSONI	Dark purplish ; hardy.
HENRY BESSAMER . .	Rich crimson, intensely blotched with black markings, and well defined; one of Mr. Waterer's new seedlings.
HESTER	Fine white, reddish-brown spots.
H. H. HUNNEWELL .	Dark rich crimson ; good habit; fine foliage ; probably hardy.
HOGARTH	Rosy-crimson ; a fine, late-blooming variety; precariously hardy.
H. W. SARGENT . . .	Crimson; enormous truss; fine habit and foliage; probably hardy.
IAGO	Rosy-violet, dark spots.
INGRAMI	Blush, blotched with lemon; fine form.
JAMES BATEMAN . .	Clear rosy-scarlet; good form; probably hardy.
JAMES NASMYTH . .	Rich mulberry, with distinct orange spot; one of Mr. Waterer's new seedlings.

JAMES McINTOSH . .	Rosy-scarlet.
J. MARSHALL BROOKS	Scarlet, with rich brown blotch; a new seedling of Mr. Waterer.
JOHN SPENCER . . .	A fine truss of rosy flowers, margined with deep pink; a late bloomer, and probably hardy.
JOHN WATERER . . .	Intense dark crimson; a fine, free-blooming variety; large flower and fine form.
JOHNSONIANUM . . .	Brilliant crimson; tender.
JOSEPH WHITWORTH .	Dark lake, with darker spots; large flowers; fine foliage.
LADY ANNETTE DE TRAFFORD	Pale rose, intensely blotched with chocolate; a new seedling of Mr. Waterer's.
LADY ARMSTRONG . .	Pale rose, beautifully spotted; probably hardy.
LADY CLERMONT . .	Rosy-scarlet, intensely blotched with black; probably hardy.
LADY DOROTHY NEVILLE.	Lavender-white, finely spotted; same as ÉTENDARD DE FLANDRES.
LADY ELEANOR CATHCART	Clear bright rose, with chocolate-crimson spots; very beautiful.
LADY EMILY PEEL . .	Bright rose, chocolate spots.
LADY FALMOUTH . .	Clear rose, deep black blotch.
LADY GODIVA . . .	White, finely spotted with ochre; large flower.
LEE'S PURPLE . . .	Dark purple; a fine bloomer; hardy, distinct, and good.
LADY FRANCES CROSSLEY	Rosy-pink or salmon.

LEFEVREANUM . . . Rich purplish - crimson; good foliage; hardy.

LEVIATHAN . . . . Blush, margined and tinged with violet; fine form and flower.

LEOPARDI . . . . . Lilac, spotted all over with chocolate.

LIMBATUM . . . . . Rosy - white, shading to pure white throat; deep rose blotch; tender. Figured in Bot. Mag. 88, t. 5311. A variety of *R. arboreum*.

LONDINENSE . . . . Crimson-purple; good form and free bloomer; precariously hardy; same as NE PLUS ULTRA.

LORD CLYDE . . . . Dark rich crimson; same as BRABANTIA.

LORD JOHN RUSSELL . Rose, intensely spotted; very showy and beautiful; tender.

LOWII . . . . . . White, distinctly spotted with orange - chocolate; tender; same as PICTUM.

LUCIDUM . . . . . Lilac, brown spots; free bloomer; beautiful foliage; tender.

LUCY NEAL . . . . Purplish - crimson, shaded to scarlet; same as GENSERIC.

MACRANTHUM . . . Rosy - blush; late bloomer; hardy and desirable.

MACULATUM GRANDI- ⎱ Dark rosy - lilac, spotted; fine
FLORUM. . . . . ⎰ form and truss; same as CURRIEANUM.

MACULATUM NIGRUM . Dark purple, spotted.

MACULATUM PURPUREUM	Light purple, deeply spotted; large truss; hardy; same as CHANCELLOR.
MACULATUM RUBRUM .	Rose, finely spotted.
MACULATUM SUPERBUM	Lilac-rose, intensely spotted with black; large and fine truss; a late bloomer.
MADAME CARVALHO .	Clear white, greenish-brown spots; fine shape and substance.
MAGNUM BONUM . .	Rosy-lilac, beautifully spotted; large flower; precariously hardy.
MARC ANTONY . . .	Lilac, brown eye; hardy.
MARGINATO PUNCTATUM	White ground, deep carmine spots. Figured in Illus. Hort. 14, t. 505.
METAPHOR	Rose; large truss; fine form.
MICHAEL WATERER .	Scarlet-crimson; fine form; very beautiful.
MILNEI	Rosy-crimson; large truss.
MINNIE	White, with large blotch of orange-chocolate; fine form and substance; remains long in bloom, one of the most striking varieties; tender. Figured in Illus. Hort. 9, t. 317.
MIRANDUM	Rose; fine foliage.
MT. BLANC . . .	White; dwarf; free blooming; tender.
MR. JOHN PENN . .	Salmon-pink, deeper edge.
MRS. FITZGERALD . .	Bright rosy-scarlet.

MRS. G. H. W. HENEAGE   Rosy-purple, white centre, fringed; remains long in bloom; probably hardy.

MRS. JOHN CLUTTON .   Splendid flower; white, yellow-spotted; of fine form and substance, remaining long in bloom; probably hardy. Figured in Florist, September, 1869.

MRS. JOHN WATERER .   Rosy-crimson, spotted; fine truss.

MRS. MILNER . . . .   Rich crimson; fine foliage and flower; probably hardy.

MRS. SAM MENDEL   .   Clear rose; distinct white ray up the centre of each petal, and beautifully spotted; one of Anthony Waterer's new seedlings.

MRS. JOSEPH SHUTTLE-⎱ Pale rose, intensely blotched;
WORTH . . . . . ⎰   new.

MRS. R. S. HOLFORD .   Rich salmon, a new color; large truss and flower; a superb Rhododendron; tender.

MRS. THOMAS BRASSEY   Clear white, margined with rosy-purple.

MRS. THOMAS WAIN   .   Pale rose, deep brown blotch; very beautiful; probably hardy.

MURILLO . . . . .   Rich crimson.

NEIGE ET CERISE . .   Snowy white, bordered with rich carmine; very beautiful; tender. Figured in Fl. des Ser. 13, t. 1391.

NEILSONI	Rosy-lake; large flower and truss.
NEREUS	Light purple, dark spots.
NE PLUS ULTRA . .	Crimson-purple; same as LONDINENSE.
NERO	Dark rosy-purple, richly spotted; fine form and truss; tender.
NIGRESCENS	Dark plum-color, almost black.
OCULISSIMUM	Rose, deeply marked.
OLD PORT.	Rich plum-color.
ONSLOWIANUM . . .	Waxy blush, yellow eye; distinct and fine; hardy.
ORNATUM	Rose; late bloomer.
ORNATISSIMUM . . .	White, bordered to delicate rose, shading almost to purple. Figured in Illus. Hort. 14, t. 530.
OTHELLO	Crimson, with mauve tinge.
PAPILIONACEUM . . .	Pale lilac, changing to white, orange spots.
PARDOLETON	Rosy-lilac, spotted; precariously hardy.
PAXTONI	Rose, deeply spotted; precariously hardy.
PELARGONIFLORUM .	White, shaded pink, red spots, and yellowish lighting. Figured in Fl. des Ser. 10, t. 1063.
PERFECTION	Blush, yellow eye; fine form.
PERRIEANUM	Light rose, finely spotted.
PERSPICUUM	White or blush.
PICTUM	White, beautifully spotted; same as LOWII.
POUSSIN	Deep rosy-crimson; same as BARCLAYANUM.

PRESIDENT VAN DEN HECKE	Light rose, beautifully spotted; precariously hardy.
PRINCE ALBERT . . .	Rich lake.
PRINCE CAMILLE DE ROHAN	Rose, deeply spotted with brownish-red, fringed. Figured in Fl. des Ser. 10, t. 1073; and Illus. Hort. 2, t. 46.
PRINCE EUGENE . . .	Blush, intense spot on the upper petal.
PRINCESS MARY OF CAMBRIDGE. . . .	White centre, edge of petals rosy-purple; fine.
PRINCE OF WALES (Young's). . . .	Brilliant rose, shaded to purple, black marking on the upper petals. Figured in Fl. Mag. pl. 177.
PRINCESS OF WALES .	Creamy white centre, bordered with violet-purple. Figured in Fl. des Ser. 18, t. 1834–5.
PURPUREUM ELEGANS .	Fine purple; hardy.
PURPUREUM CRISPUM .	Purple, fringed; hardy.
PURPUREUM GRANDIFLORUM	Purple; large truss and flower; hardy.
PURITY	White, faint yellow eye.
RAPHAEL	Spotted crimson; large flower.
REEDIANUM	Bright cherry-red; tender.
ROSABEL	Pale rose; fine foliage and habit; probably hardy.
ROSEUM ELEGANS . .	Rose; very hardy.
ROSEUM GRANDIFLORUM	Rose; late bloomer; hardy.
ROSEUM PICTUM . . .	Rose, yellow eye; tender.
ROSEUM SUPERBUM . .	Light rose; large truss and flower; hardy.
R. S. FIELD	Scarlet; very fine; probably hardy.

RUBENS . . . . . .   Clear rose; same as DUKE OF
                         NORFOLK.

SALMONO ROSEUM . .   Rosy - salmon, deeply spotted;
                         delicate and pretty. Figured
                         in Illus. Hort. 12, t. 437.

SCHILLER . . . . .   Bluish-purple, dark black spots.

SCIPIO . . . . . .   Rose, deep spot.

SHERWOODIANUM . .   Light rose, dark spots.

SIDNEY HERBERT . .   Bright crimson, with blotch of
                         black spots.

SIGISMUND RUCKER .   Rich dark puce, new and fine.

SIR CHARLES NAPIER   Rose, beautifully spotted; fine
                         shape.

SIR ISAAC NEWTON .   Claret - crimson, shaded and
                         spotted; same as BLATTEUM.

SIR JAMES CLARK . .   Dark crimson, shaded with pur-
                         ple.

SIR JOHN THWAITES .   Deep scarlet, distinctly blotched
                         with yellow; a new seedling
                         of Mr. Waterer's.

SIR ROBERT PEEL . .   Bright crimson, dark spots.

SIR THOMAS SEABRIGHT   Rich purple, distinct bronze
                         blotch; remaining long in
                         flower.

SIR WILLIAM ARM-
    STRONG . . . . .   Crimson; fine truss and flower.

SOUVENIR DE JEAN ⎫   Red, with yellowish - green
    BYLS . . . . . . ⎭   blotch on the upper petal.
                         Figured in Illus. Hort. 9,
                         t. 326.

SPECIOSUM . . . . .   Light pink; hardy.

SPLENDENS . . . .   Rose; very good.

STAMFORDIANUM. . .   Dark pink, with deep purple or
                         black spots. Figured in Fl.
                         des Ser. 14, t. 1428.

STANDARD OF FLANDERS   Lavender-white, finely spotted; same as LADY DOROTHY NEVILLE and ÉTENDARD DE FLANDRES.

STANDISHII . . . .   Rosy-purple, spotted.

STELLA . . . . . .   Pale rose, deep chocolate blotch; very distinct and showy; probably hardy.

SULTANA . . . . .   White, reddish-brown spots.

SURPRISE . . . . .   Lilac, chocolate blotch.

THE GRAND ARAB . .   Brilliant crimson; fine shape.

THE SUN OF AUSTER- LITZ . . . . . .   Crimson - scarlet; same as BRILLIANT.

THE GEM . . . . .   Light blush, tinged with pink.

THE QUEEN . . . .   Blush, changing to white.

THE WARRIOR . . .   Rosy - crimson ; fine form and foliage.

TITIAN . . . . . .   Light rosy-scarlet; very beautiful; tender.

TOWARDII . . . . .   Rosy-lilac ; beautiful form.

VANDYKE . . . . .   Rosy - crimson ; late bloomer ; very fine ; hardy.

VERSCHAFFELTII . .   Pale lavender - pink, deeply spotted on the upper petals. Figured in Illus. Hort. 9, t. 317.

VESUVIUS . . . . .   Crimson - scarlet, black spots; large truss.

VESTITUM COCCINEUM .   Very showy crimson.

VICTORIA (Piñce's) . .   Claret-crimson.

VICTORIA . . . . .   Plum-color.

WILLIAM DOWNING .   Rich dark puce, finely blotched; remaining long in bloom; a magnificent plant in flower and foliage. Figured in Fl. des Ser. 17, t. 734–5.

The foregoing list is a selection of the most approved varieties. Some of them are new kinds that have not been proved, but which promise to surpass all older varieties.

Of the list of two hundred and forty-six, we have more than one hundred now in our garden. Many of those marked "tender" have been grown and discarded as unsuited to our climate.

There is probably not one of the varieties mentioned which could not be successfully grown in the open air south of Philadelphia; and a large proportion would succeed further north.

With such a collection to choose from, what garden should be without Rhododendrons?

The following lists may prove useful in selecting: —

For one Rhododendron, perfectly hardy, and which combines good foliage, fine flower, and free growing and blooming habit, —

Everestianum.

For three hardy kinds, add, —

Album grandiflorum and Purpureum grandiflorum.

For six, add, —

Coriaceum, Grandiflorum, and Roseum elegans.

For twelve, add, —

Album elegans.	Hannibal.
Lee's Dark Purple.	Giganteum.
Delicatissimum.	Gloriosum.

For twenty-four, add, —

Purpureum clegans.
Roseum grandiflorum.
Bicolor.
Cœlestinum.
Macranthum.
Cœlestinum pictum.

Album.
Columbus.
Candidissimum (Parsons).
Purpureum crispum.
Cunningham's Dwarf White.
Speciosum.

List of eighteen very fine Rhododendrons, which will generally prove hardy : —

Archimedes.
Atrosanguineum.
Barclayanum.
Blandyanum.
Brayanum.
Curricanum.
Hendersoni.
Lefevreanum.
Maculatum purpureum.

Ne Plus Ultra.
Onslowianum.
Pardoleton.
Paxtoni.
Rubens.
Standard of Flanders.
Azureum,
Cœrulescens.
Roseum superbum.

List of twenty-five magnificent varieties, requiring cellar protection in winter : —

Aclandianum.
Alarm.
Broughtoni.
Bylsianum.
Concessum.
Desdemona.
Elfrida.
Fastuosum fl. pl.
Fleur de Marie.
Lady Cathcart.
Lady Crossley.
Limbatum.

Lord John Russell.
Maculatum superbum.
Minnie.
Neige et Cerise.
Nero.
Pictum.
Princess Mary of Cambridge.
Sir Charles Napier.
Sidney Herbert.
Titian.
Towardii.
Vandyck.

William Downing.

List of Late Blooming Varieties: —

Barclayanum.	John Spencer.
Hogarth.	Maculatum superbum.
Roseum grandiflorum.	Ornatum.
Hannibal.	Vandyck.
Francis Dickson.	William Downing.

Macranthum.

List of New Varieties, which will probably prove hardy: —

Caractacus.	Lady Clermont.
Charles Bagley.	Edward S. Rand.
Charles Dickens.	Mrs. Heneage.
Guido.	Stella.
H. H. Hunnewell.	Rosabel.
H. W. Sargent.	Purity.
James Bateman.	Mrs. John Clutton.
John Spencer.	Mrs. Milner.
Lady Armstrong.	Mrs. Wain.

R. S. Field.

List of twenty-five very distinct varieties: —

Barclayanum.	Minnie.
Brayanum.	Mrs. John Clutton.
Lord John Russell.	Mrs. R. S. Holford.
Concessum.	Neige et Cerise.
Cruentum.	Nero.
Elfrida.	Nigrescens.
Fastuosum fl. pl.	Onslowianum.
H. W. Sargent.	President van den Hecke.
Stella.	Hannibal.
Lady Clermont.	Titian.
Lady Frances Crossley.	Towardii.
Maculatum superbum.	William Downing.

Lady Cathcart.

List of varieties for Standards:—

Everestianum.	Brayanum.
Roseum elegans.	Victoria.
Minnie.	Concessum.
Lady Cathcart.	Fastuosum fl. pl.
William Downing.	Archimedes.
Maculatum superbum.	Barclayanum.

Roseum pictum.

PART III.

OTHER "AMERICAN PLANTS.'

PART III.

OTHER "AMERICAN PLANTS."

THE greater part of the plants enumerated in this portion of our work belong to the same natural family as the Rhododendron (Ericaceæ), and thrive best with the same treatment. In English catalogues they are included under the general name of "American plants;" and, although some are not natives of America, we adopt the popular name as most familiar.

They are especially adapted for combination with Rhododendrons, and afford a wide range of color in bloom, and a great variety of foliage. Among them we find many plants combining symmetry of form, beauty and fragrance of flower, and easy culture. Some are rarely seen; but all are easily obtained, and well repay the care necessary to have them in perfection.

THE AZALEA.

This genus is nearly related to Rhododendron, and indeed by some botanists has been included in it.   Early volumes of some illustrated horticultural works figure all Azaleas as Rhododendrons.

The genus Azalea has also been extended by other botanists so as to include many plants which the best authorities now give to other genera.   As now defined, the genus is confined to about twenty species, natives of Asia and North America, all shrubs, mostly with large showy flowers, which, both from their beauty and fragrance, are popular ornaments of our gardens and shrubberies.

The tender species are well-known greenhouse plants, and both these and the hardy kinds have in cultivation developed many very beautiful varieties.

Those that are hardy thrive best in Rhododendron soil, and need the same general culture as prescribed for Rhododendrons.   They grow freely, flower profusely, and need only to be kept from drought to do well.   They are all deciduous, and therefore, where a mass of foliage is wanted for the winter, should not be mixed with Rhododendrons.   We prefer to plant them in masses by themselves; although when in bloom, and during the summer, they combine well with other American plants.   As specimens and standards, they are very handsome; always blooming well, and forming a conspicuous feature in the garden.   All the species are propagated easily by inarching, grafting, or by cuttings of the half-ripened shoots, which root readily under a bell-glass in sandy peat.   The hardy kinds are also increased by layers, in the same manner as Rhododendrons.   New varieties are obtained from seed, which should be sown in sandy peat, as directed for Rhododendrons.

The tender species are evergreen plants, requiring the protection of a cool greenhouse in winter. In summer they should be set out of doors, in a partially shaded situation.

All the species bear pruning well, and may be cut to any required shape. In habit they vary greatly, some naturally being of fine form, and others requiring severe pruning. The foliage is not ornamental, being usually dull or rusty green; but when in bloom the plants are such a mass of flower that the leaves are not noticed.

For forcing in the greenhouse, all the species are well adapted; and there are no better or more easily grown parlor plants than the varieties of tender Azaleas.

Many hybrids have been produced by fertilization between the Azalea and the Rhododendron. Many of these we have already described: they vary greatly in habit, foliage, and flower, according as they partake of the nature of either parent. The number is very large, and is yearly increasing. The species are: —

AZALEA ARBORESCENS.

A tall shrub, native of the Middle and Southern States, with large, fragrant, rose-colored flowers. The foliage is smooth above, glaucous below, and ornamental. The flowers appear in June, after the leaves.

We have been unable to find a figure of this species.

AZALEA NUDIFLORA.

A well-known shrub, native of swamps, from Massachusetts southward; producing a profusion of showy flowers, which vary much in color, early in May.

The common names are Wild Honeysuckle and Pinxter Flower, the latter from its blooming about Whit-Sunday.

The flowers appear before the leaves, often in such abundance as to cover the whole plant. In the wild state they are found of every shade, from purple to blush-white. Seedlings vary greatly, and in cultivation numerous hybrids have been produced, affording a wide range of color.

The following varieties of this species are very fine: *Versicolor*, do. *grandiflora, mirabilis, carnea delicatissima, colorata. incarnata superba, coccinea,* do. *major, incana, Coburghii.* All have scarlet, pink, or blush flowers, and are perfectly hardy.

AZALEA VISCOSA.

This species is the well-known " Swamp Honey-suckle," so common in low swamps, damp, shady woods, and by road-sides.

It forms a tall shrub, with dark green leaves, and bears in the latter part of June and July an abundance of clammy, white, deliciously fragrant flowers, sometimes tinged with deep rose.

It thrives in cultivation, not requiring a wet soil, but growing and blooming freely if the roots are not allowed to dry up. From its fragrance and late blooming, it is a desirable plant. There are numerous varieties, and this species is the parent of many hybrids. All are hardy.

Some of the best are: *rubescens*, do. *grandiflora*, *floribunda*, *penicillata*, do. *picta*.

AZALEA GLAUCA

Is only a variety of *A. viscosa*, with pale glaucous foliage; not uncommon.

AZALEA NITIDA

Is also a variety of *A. viscosa*, of dwarf habit, with dark green, shining leaves, and white, clammy flowers, tinged with pink.

AZALEA CALENDULACEA.

A shrub, growing from five to ten feet high, with hairy leaves and large, flame-colored or orange, scentless flowers; native of the Middle and Southern States. It is common in gardens, is hardy, and flowers freely in May, the blossoms appearing with the leaves. There are many varieties, of which we may mention: *Morterii*, *fulgida*, *calendulacea coccinea*, do. *crocea*, do. *elegans*, do. *eximia*, do. *flammea*, do. *superba*, *ignescens*, *triumphans*.

AZALEA PONTICA.

A native of Asia Minor and the Caucasus, forming a tall shrub, with bright yellow flowers in the species, which in the numerous varieties are found of every shade, from yellow to copper or orange, white or striped.

This species seeds freely ; and from it, by hybridizing with the American species, innumerable seedlings have been raised. Much attention has been paid to thus crossing the species in Belgium, especially in the neighborhood of Ghent ; whence all hardy Azaleas have come to be known as " Belgian, or Ghent Azaleas."

These seedlings are generally hardy, although some of the lighter-colored varieties have proved tender with us : and some lose their flower-buds in severe winters, although the wood is not injured.

Some of the best varieties referred to this species are: *ardens, aurantia,* do. *major, candida, coronaria, cuprea, pontica alba, carnea, compacta, conspicua, delicatissima, grandiflora, grandidissima, imperialis, mutabilis, multiflora pallida, macrantha, princeps, sulphurea,* do. *grandiflora,* do. do. *nova.*

There are innumerable other hybrid varieties in nurserymen's catalogues, and every year gives us an increased number.

To the above lists we may add, as desirable: *Adelaide, alta-clarense, aurea speciosa* and *grandiflora, Clireana, autumnalis, concinna, decus hortorum, elegantissima, Napoleon III., flammeola incarnata, fama, gloriosa, Marie Verschaffelt, nitens, Ne Plus Ultra, ornata rosea, praenitens, violæ odorata.*

Those who are not familiar with the flower will find fine varieties figured in Bot. Mag. 28, t. 27, 17, t. 1402, 31, t. 51–60. 16, t. 1366–67 : Illus. Hort. t. 75, 209, 415 : Fl. des Serres, 1298, 1306–7.

Mr. Anthony Waterer, of the Knap Hill Nursery, near Woking, Surrey, England, has been very successful in raising seedling Azaleas, and within the past few years has produced some varieties which are far superior to any before raised. This has been accomplished by crossing the best hardy kinds with *Azalea sinensis*, a Chinese species, with large, golden, Rhododendron-like flowers.

These new varieties are thus described in Mr. Waterer's catalogue of the present year : —

AMŒNA . . . . . . Delicate rose, with rich buff spot.

BESSIE HOLDAWAY . Bright rose, clear bronze spot.

CUPREA . . . . . . Coppery - orange, shaded with salmon.

FULGIDA . . . . . Bright fiery-orange, deeper in the centre.

NANCY WATERER . . The finest of all the yellows, rich and deep in color; large in size and perfect in form.

OCHROLEUCA . . . . Pale straw - color, with golden spot.

PRIMULINA . . . . Delicate primrose-yellow.

PULCHRA . . . . Shaded rose, with orange blotch.

SINENSIS ROSEA . . . Pale, shaded rose.

STRAMINEA . . . . An extremely delicate tint of straw-color.

SULPHUREA . . . . Sulphur-yellow, with deep yellow blotch.

Figures of Nancy Waterer and Bessie Holdaway are given in the "Florist" for May, 1869.

DOUBLE HARDY AZALEAS.

These are very beautiful and desirable, as they are very showy and remain long in bloom.

They are perfectly hardy, having stood the last four winters with us; grow freely and flower abundantly.

The varieties are: Maja, Van Houtte, Ophire, Dr. Streiter, Heroine, Bartolo Lazaris, Narcissiflora, Leibnitz, Graaf von Meran.

AZALEA AMŒNA.

This is a charming little Chinese species, usually grown as a greenhouse plant, but perfectly hardy.

The flowers are purple, produced in the "hose in hose" form, in gardening parlance; that is, with a double corolla. The plant was found by Mr. Fortune, near Shanghae, and, as we have it in cultivation, is evidently a garden variety of some unknown species. The flower resembles that of *Rhododendron dauricum*, and, like that, is produced in very early spring, almost too early with us. The foliage is evergreen.

Figured in Pax. Fl. G. pl. 89; Lem. Jar. 4, t. 329; Bot. Mag. 79, t. 4728.

AZALEA SINENSIS.

A Chinese species, with large, yellow-orange flowers, to which we have already had occasion to refer as one of the parents of the hybrid yellow Rhododendrons, and of Mr. Waterer's new hardy Azaleas. The flowers are scentless, and only resemble those of *A. pontica* in color. A very showy plant.

Figured in Lodd. Cab. t. 885.

Variety ALBA, with white flowers, is figured in Illus. Hort. t. 563.

AZALEA SQUAMATA.

A Chinese species, with small, lavender-purple flowers, with crimson spots, produced before the leaves; probably not hardy.

Figured in Bot. Reg. 33, t. 3 .

AZALEA OBTUSA.

Also a Chinese species, with small, deep-red spotted flowers and evergreen foliage. The flowers are fragrant. Coming from the north of China it may be hardy.

Figured in Bot. Reg. 32, t. 37.

AZALEA LEDIFOLIA.

This species, also known as *Azalea indica alba*, is the well-known white Azalea of our greenhouses. The foliage is rough, small, and not ornamental; the flowers large, white, and fragrant. It is the parent of innumerable varieties, which are far superior to the parent.

Figured in Bot. Mag. t. 2901.

The purple Azalea, generally known as *A. phœ-nicea*, is a variety of this species.

Figured in Bot. Mag. t. 3239.

AZALEA INDICA.

This species is the parent of all the so-called "greenhouse Azaleas." It is a native of China and Japan, with very showy scarlet, red, or white flowers; but has sported into numerous varieties, some of which are among the most attractive of greenhouse plants. None of them are hardy.

Those who are not familiar with this flower will find very beautiful figures of fine varieties in Floral Mag. pl. 63, 59, 25, 39, 14, 113, 104, 193, 231, 201, 268, 303, 395; Illus. Hort. t. 8. 20. 38, 65, 90, 130, 136, 170, 178. 182, 267, 302, 288, 340, 342, 428, 478, 512; Fl. des Ser. t. 1618–22, 1654. 1572, 1567, 1365, 1334, 1301-2-3, 1060, 1180, 1157, 1243; Hen. Illus. Bou. pl. 23.

AZALEA OVATA.

A small, pretty species, with pale purple flowers, and small, shining green foliage; native of China.

Figured in Bot. Mag. t. 5064.

AZALEA OCCIDENTALIS

Is the Californian species. The flowers are large, white, marked with yellow; a very showy plant, and probably hardy.

Figured in Bot. Mag. t. 5005; and Fl. des Ser. 14, t. 1432.

The Rhodora.

There is but one species of this genus, *R. canadensis;* a low, deciduous shrub, not uncommon in New England, and often found so plentifully as to cover acres.

The leaves are deciduous: the flowers of every shade from purple to pure white, blooming in clusters, before the leaves, in early May.

It is a pretty plant, readily obtained, of easy culture, and does well in any moist loam.

It thrives wonderfully in a Rhododendron-bed, and is well worthy of the position from its showy, abundant, and early bloom.

Figured in Bot. Mag. 14, t. 474.

The Loiseleuria.

The only species is *L. procumbens*, sometimes known as *Azalea procumbens*. It is a small, evergreen shrub, a native of high latitudes, on mountains, both in this country and Europe. The flowers are small, white or pink, in terminal clusters.

It would probably do well on the border of a Rhododendron-bed.

Figured in Lodd. Cab. t. 762; Bax. Brit. Bot. 6. t. 463.

The Kalmia.

These well-known plants, the "Mountain Laurel" of our woods, are fit companions for Rhododendrons, thriving under the same treatment, and harmonizing well with them, both in foliage and flower.

Their culture is very simple, being only to plant them in moist soil, and leave them to grow. While they will bear pruning, they seldom need it; for, if not crowded, they form symmetrical bushes themselves. They are propagated by layers or from seed, in the same manner as Rhododendrons.

They are perfectly hardy, although in exposed situations the foliage sometimes gets browned in winter.

No insect attacks them, and they are subject to no diseases.

A mass of the large-flowered Kalmia in full bloom is a beautiful sight, and the smaller species are all attractive and pretty.

No words can describe the beauty of this plant on the mountains of the Middle States, where it covers acres, and sheets whole hillsides with pink and white. Even in New England there are places where it grows in great abundance, but it does not flower as freely as further south.

The plant is popularly known as "Mountain Laurel," in distinction from the "Great Laurel" (*Rhododendron maximum*); also as "Spoonwood" and "Calico Bush."

The common small species is called Sheep Laurel, or Lambkill.

The foliage of all the species is evergreen, but only in *Kalmia latifolia* is ornamental.

Kalmia latifolia.

This is the most showy species, and is one of the most ornamental of our indigenous plants. It is a tall shrub, sometimes attaining the height of ten feet. In cultivation, however, it is seldom more than half that height, and grows thick and bushy. The foliage is dark shining green, large and ornamental.

The flowers vary from pure white to deep pink, and thus constitute the varieties of some nursery catalogues. Seedlings vary much in size of the flower, in floriferous qualities, and in form of the corymbs of bloom; some bearing close, compact masses, others having them very loose and straggling.

Although a native of our woods, the cheapest and easiest mode of procuring plants is to import them from England, where they are raised from seed in large quantities. Nice, bushy plants, about a foot high, cost only twenty-five dollars per hundred landed here, and, as they grow rapidly, soon form large plants.

Kalmias mass well with Rhododendrons, and, as they bloom somewhat later, serve to keep up the period of bloom in the bed. We prefer them, however, as specimen plants, or in clumps by themselves.

Figured in Bot. Mag. 5, pl. 175; Michaux, Arb. 3. pl. 5; Big. Med. pl. 13.

Variety myrtifolia is a dwarf-growing plant, with small, shining leaves; very pretty for the borders of beds.

Kalmia angustifolia

Is by no means a popular plant, from the foliage being poisonous to sheep; whence the common name of "Lambkill." It is, however, very pretty, and improves greatly on acquaintance. The foliage is narrow, dull green, glaucous below, and not ornamental. The flowers vary from pale pink to the deepest red.

By a little search in the fields in the season of bloom, many varieties, differing greatly in color, foliage, and growth, may be obtained. The plant is too pretty to be neglected, and were it less common would be highly esteemed.

Planted on the border of a Rhododendron-bed, it increases rapidly by suckers, and never fails to flower freely.

Figured in Bot. Mag. 10, t. 331; and in Lodd. Cab. pl. 502.

Kalmia glauca.

A charmingly pretty species, and the earliest to bloom, the flowers expanding in early May. The foliage is narrow, evergreen, whitish below; the flowers large, rose-colored, in terminal corymbs.

While in its native bogs, the plant is a low, straggling shrub.

We receive it from England in neat, pretty, symmetrical plants, which always come out of the cases in full bloom. It is not so easy of culture as the other species, and is very liable to die off.

The varieties *stricta*, *superba*, and *rosmarinifolia*, only differ from the species in size and color of flower, or in foliage.

Figured in Bot. Mag. 5, t. 177; Lodd. Cab. t. 1508.

KALMIA HIRSUTA.

This species is a native of pine barren swamps of the Southern States. The foliage is small; the flowers large, rose-colored, solitary, produced in the axils of the leaves. This plant would probably prove of difficult cultivation and be tender in the Northern States.

Figured in Bot. Mag. 4, t. 138; Lodd. Cab. t. 1058.

KALMIA CUNEATA.

This species, which is a native of the mountains of Carolina, we have never seen. It is said to be deciduous; and to bear white flowers, red at the bottom, in few-flowered, lateral corymbs.

THE LEDUM.

This plant, familiarly known as "Labrador Tea," is by no means uncommon in low mountain bogs. The foliage is rusty, pleasantly fragrant; the flowers in large, terminal clusters, white and very showy. All the species thrive on the borders of Rhododendron-beds, for which place their low growth adapts them. They bloom in May, and flower freely and regularly. All are perfectly hardy.

LEDUM PALUSTRE.

A low shrub, with linear leaves with revolute margins; flowers white. A native of Canada and the north of Europe.

Figured in Lodd. Cab. t. 560; Bax. Brit. Bot. 6, p. 508.

L. DECUMBENS is a prostrate variety from the far North.

LEDUM LATIFOLIUM.

Altogether a larger plant in every way. Leaves broad; flowers large, white. The most showy species, and well worth cultivating.

Figured in Lodd. Cab. t. 534.

We have in our garden a plant received under the name of *Ledum angustifolium*, which seems to be intermediate between these two species.

L. canadense, figured in Lodd. Cab. t. 1049, does not appear to differ in flower from other species.

The plants sometimes known as *L. buxifolium* and *thymifolium* are now referred to *Leiophyllum*.

THE LEIOPHYLLUM.

A charming little evergreen, with small, shining leaves, somewhat resembling a myrtle; whence the popular name, "Sand Myrtle."

The only species is *L. buxifolium*, a native of New Jersey and southward, but perfectly hardy with us at Glen Ridge.

The flowers are small, white, or tinged with pink on the ends of the branches, in close corymbs, and in the latter part of May completely cover the plant. At other seasons the evergreen foliage is very neat and pretty. A border of this plant around a mass of Rhododendrons, Kalmias, or Azaleas, is very effective.

Figured in Lodd. Cab. 52, as *Ledum buxifolium*.

The plant known as *L. thymifolium* is a variety, with smaller foliage, equally ornamental and desirable. This plant is also known as *Ammyrsine*.

THE MENZIESIA.

A genus of small shrubs, not very ornamental, but desirable in a collection. The foliage is deciduous, and resembles that of an Azalea; the flowers are small, greenish-white or brownish-purple.

The species is *M. ferruginea*, a native of North-western America, of which the variety *globularis* is found plentifully on mountains in Virginia.

Figured in Bot. Mag. 38, t. 1571; and the variety in Hook. Bor. Am. 132.

THE PHYLLODOCE.

The plant known in florist's catalogues as *Menziesia cœrulea* is a charming little plant, resembling a Heath both in foliage and flower; a native of North-western

6*

America, of the White Mountains, and some parts of Europe. It is very ornamental, and will thrive in cool, moist soil. The flowers are bluish-purple, nodding, and charmingly pretty. The proper name of the plant is *Phyllodoce taxifolia.* There is also another species, *P.* or *M. empetriformis,* with pale red flowers.

See figures in Lodd. Cab. t. 164, and Bot. Mag. t. 3176.

The species of *Daboecia,* pretty heath-like plants with showy flowers, but not hardy with us, are sometimes called *Menzietia.*

THE CALLUNA.

This plant, the " Heather " of Europe, is hardy enough to endure our winters. Blooming in July, when flowers are not plenty, it forms a most attractive border to a clump of evergreens. The plant is low-growing, with heath-like foliage, and when in bloom is a mass of flower. The species *C. vulgaris* is a native of Europe, but has been found growing wild near Boston, the locality being such as to leave little doubt as to its being indigenous. The flowers are rose-colored : but there are garden varieties of every shade from red to white, one with double flowers and one with golden foliage. All these are easily grown along the borders of Rhododendron-beds, and with a slight covering of pine-needles in winter escape entirely uninjured.

They can be imported for about three dollars a dozen.

Figured in Eng. Bot. 15, t. 1013; and in Bax. Brit. Bot. 1, t. 76.

THE GYPSOCALLIS.

The hardiest of the "Heaths," as the plant is always found in catalogues as *Erica herbacea*. It is a native of Central Europe, but with us has proved hardy in all exposures, the only care taken being to cover the plant with pine-needles in winter; as in our experience, while no degree of cold injured the plant, the flower-buds were killed when the mercury fell below zero. The species to which we specially refer is *G. carnea*. This little plant is low-growing, like the Heather; and, like it, is suited for the borders of Rhododendron-beds. It blooms in the early days of spring, opening its flowers with the crocuses in April, and giving to the bees the first promise of summer.

The flowers are pale red or whitish, and completely cover the plant. By growing it in every position, from very sunny to very shady, a succession of bloom may be obtained for weeks. We regard this as one of the most valuable of spring flowers.

Figured in Bot. Mag. t. 11: Lodd. Cab. t. 1452.

The other species of *Gypsocallis* are not hardy in New England, although they are often grown as greenhouse plants.

THE CASSIOPE.

C. hypnoides is a rarely beautiful plant, with moss-like foliage and lovely red and white flowers. It is a native of Lapland and Siberia, and is found on the tops of the mountains of New England.

Although hardy, it is very difficult of cultivation: the best place for it would be in a shady bed of sandy peat.

Figured in Bot. Mag. t. 2936.

Another species, *C. tetragona*, also a native of high northern latitudes, is very difficult to keep in cultivation. It is a beautiful plant, with large, drooping, white, bell-shaped flowers.

Figured in Bot. Mag. t. 3181.

These plants were formerly known as *Andromeda*. There are other species not in cultivation.

The Arctostaphylos.

A small, trailing plant, very generally distributed over America and Europe. The common name is "Bearberry." The flowers are small, white, tinged with red, very pretty; the leaves small, box-like, evergreen. It does well in peat, or will thrive in any sandy loam, and is a good plant for rock-work.

Figured in Wood. Med. Bot. t. 70; Bax. Brit. Bot. 6, t. 502.

A. alpina is a deciduous species, with pure white flowers and black berries; a native of high mountains, both in Europe and America. Like the last, the stems are trailing; and it is a suitable plant for covering the ground.

Figured in Eng. Bot. t. 2030.

A. glauca is the "Mazaneta" of California, and varies in size from a tall shrub in the low country to a very low creeping bush far up above the snowline. The flowers are pink and very handsome, the foliage clear glaucous green, the bush red. Altogether the plant is very ornamental, and if hardy will prove a great addition to our shrubbery. We have plants sent from California now on trial.

THE EPIGÆA.

There is but one species, *E. repens*, the "Trailing Arbutus," "Ground Laurel," or "May Flower," almost too well known to need description. Neat in habit and foliage, deliciously fragrant in flower, and blooming at a season when it is especially attractive, this charming plant is seldom found in cultivation. We are told "it cannot be grown in gardens," yet nothing is easier.

Obtain good plants, either from the woods or by importation, in early spring, or any time after August; plant them in your Rhododendron-bed, and your work is done. They will increase, carpet the ground, give you flower year after year, and ask you for no attention.

There is not in the whole floral kingdom a more attractive flower, and it loses none of its wild-wood beauty when we take it to our homes.

The flowers vary much in size and color, and, in planting, the largest and most highly colored should be selected. Plants may also be raised from seed.

Figured in And. Bot. Rep. 102; Lodd. Cab. t. 160; Bot. Reg. 3, t. 201; Sweet, Fl. G. 2, t. 384.

The Gaultheria.

A genus of low, shrubby plants, with neat flow-ers and showy berries, particularly adapted for cov-ering the surface of the ground, or for planting under trees, where little else will grow. They need no special culture beyond being planted in sandy peat, or open loamy soil; and propagate readily by suckers.

Gaultheria procumbens.

This pretty little species is the well-known "Check-erberry" of our woods, and produces the aromatic red berries so often seen in the markets. The stem is slender, creeping, never more than a few inches high. The leaves are evergreen, shining, and strongly aromatic to the taste; the flowers are pinkish-white, nodding. This plant is especially suitable for covering the surface of Rhododendron-beds, and is ornamental in foliage, flower, and fruit. The best way is to transplant them from the woods. A few set here and there will rapidly spread and cover the surface, doing no injury to the larger plants.

Figured in And. Rep. 2, t. 116; Bot. Mag. 45, t. 1966; Lodd. Cab. t. 82; Barton, Med. 15; Big. Med. 22.

Gaultheria Shallon.

A fine species from the north-western coast of America. The leaves are large, coarse, dull green; the flowers pinkish-white, very showy; the berries purplish-black, edible.

This plant in its native habitat grows in dense forests, and is thus adapted for planting under the shade of trees. In height it varies from a few inches to two feet, but is usually very low-growing, creeping along the surface and increasing rapidly by underground stems.

We are sorry to say that this beautiful species has not proved hardy with us at Glen Ridge : of a large number of plants set out a few years since, only a few survive, and these are in bad health. For some years they grew, flowered, and fruited freely ; but a winter when the mercury fell to ten degrees below zero was too severe for them, although a covering of pine-needles would probably have saved them. We strongly advise the introduction and extensive planting of this species. Plants can be bought in England for a shilling each : they transplant easily ; and wherever they prove hardy, they will be found to merit our recommendation.

Figured in Bot. Mag. 55, t. 2843 ; Bot. Reg. 17, t. 1411 ; Lodd. Cab. t. 1372.

There are other species of *Gaultheria*, but they are not in cultivation.

THE CHIOGENES.

A pretty little creeping shrub, with slender stems, close-set, evergreen leaves, inconspicuous flowers, and showy, white, aromatic berries. The species is *C. hispidula*, and is well worthy a place in some sheltered portion of the Rhododendron-bed, where it will trail over the surface, grow, flower, and fruit freely.   It is one of those natives of the wild woods which we are always charmed to find in cultivation.

Plants could easily be procured from our northern woods.

Figured in Torr. N. Y. 68; also in Pursh, Fl. 13, as *Gaultheria serpyllifolia*.

The Linnæa.

All the plants we have thus far described belong to the same family as the Rhododendron (Ericaceæ). The pretty little *Linnæa borealis*, so well adapted for covering the soil in shrubberies, is one of the Honeysuckle family (Caprifoliaceæ). It is a charming plant, with pretty evergreen foliage and delicate pink, fragrant flowers.

It is a common plant in northern woods; and we mind us of localities where it fringes the roadsides for miles, carpeting the ground under the spreading firs and hemlocks. It is impatient of drought, or of much sun, but will thrive well in a Rhododendron-bed.

Figured in Lodd. Cab. t. 183; Bax. Brit. Bot. 5, 340.

The Mitchella.

Another creeping evergreen, commonly called "Partridge" or "Twin Berry;" botanically, *M. repens*. It is very common in woods, and always beautiful, whether clothed with the lovely pink and white flowers or sparkling with scarlet berries.

It is easily procured, is very amenable to cultivation, and is well worthy a place in the garden. It belongs to the Madder family (Rubiaceæ).

Figured in Lodd. Cab. t. 979; and Barton, Fl. 3, t. 95.

THE EMPETRUM.

A plant of the Crowberry family (Empetraceæ), much resembling a heath, and worthy a place in the collection. It is not an uncommon Alpine on the summits of mountains; and is abundant on the island in Frenchman's Bay, off Mt. Desert, covering the ground and trailing over the cliffs.

The foliage is dark green and rather sombre, the flowers inconspicuous, the berries black and ornamental.

Botanically, the plant is *E. nigrum*, or Black Crowberry.

Figured in Eng. Bot. 8, t. 526; and Bax. Brit. Bot. 6, p. 469.

THE VACCINEUM.

The only plant of this genus desirable for cultivation in the garden is the Cowberry (*V. Vitis-Idæa*), a low-growing species, with dark green, shining foliage, pretty pink flowers, and showy red berries. As a plant for covering the surface, it is well worthy a place, growing freely and requiring no care.

In Maine, where this plant is very abundant, the berries are used as cranberries, and are quite palatable.

Figured in Lodd. Cab. t. 1023; Bax. Brit. Bot. 5, t. 383.

Variety MAJUS is larger in all its parts.
Figured in Lodd. Cab. t. 616.

V. OXYCOCCUS and MACROCARPUS are our small and large cranberries, both found plentifully growing wild, and the latter sometimes cultivated for market. Though naturally growing in bogs, a wet soil is not essential to them, as they do well in any good loam. The flowers and fruit of both are very pretty.

V. STAMINEUM, the Deerberry, with deciduous foliage, greenish-white flowers, and large, greenish fruit, is sometimes found in cultivation, and is not uncommon in the wild state in dry woods.

The Leucothoe.

A genus containing two of our most beautiful flowering shrubs, without which no collection of American plants can be complete, and which add greatly to the attraction of the shrubbery. They are hardy plants, doing well in Rhododendron soil, and require no special culture.
They are commonly known as *Andromeda*.

Leucothoe floribunda.

This elegant species is a native of the Southern States, on the mountains, but is generally hardy with us. The foliage is evergreen, rather small, dark green, and very ornamental; the flowers white, in panicles at the ends of the branches. The buds form in the summer, and are very conspicuous all winter, opening in early spring; the white flowers contrast beautifully with the dark foliage. A mass of this plant is a most attractive feature in the garden. As the buds are a little liable to be winter-killed with us, and the foliage sometimes gets browned, we generally protect our plants by placing over them a few evergreen boughs, with which covering they pass the winter uninjured, although in a very exposed situation, and every spring reward us by abundance of bloom. A bed of this plant, edged with the hardy heath (*Gypsocallis*), is very handsome, both plants blooming at the same time, and contrasting well in color.

In catalogues this plant is called *Andromeda floribunda*, and, botanically, is more properly referred to that genus.

Figured in Bot. Reg. 10, t. 807; and Bot. Mag. t. 1566; Pax. Mag. 4, p. 101.

LEUCOTHOE CATESBÆI.

A very showy plant, and somewhat hardier than the last described. The foliage is large, serrate, coriaceous, and evergreen; the flowers white, in long, drooping racemes. This species is ornamental, both in the mass or as a specimen plant: we grow it most successfully both ways, and regard it as one of the most desirable American plants. Its height is from one to three feet; and the slender branches, drooping with the weight of the flowers, are extremely showy. It is very hardy, never winter-killed, and never fails to flower abundantly. It thrives in a rich loam, but is impatient of drought: we grow it in beds of peaty loam, in a northern exposure; but if the roots are not allowed to dry, it will stand the full sunshine. A native of Virginia, and southward along the mountains. Known also as *Andromeda Catesbæi* and *spinulosa*, and as *L. spinulosa*.

Figured in Bot. Mag. t. 1955; Lodd. Cab. t. 1320.

LEUCOTHOE AXILLARIS.

A pretty species, but by no means so showy a plant as those we have described. The flowers are white, in axillary spikes or racemes. A native of the low country of Virginia and southward, and probably tender in New England.

Figured as *Andromeda axillaris* in Bot. Mag. t. 2357.

There are other species, some of which are tender; and others, although hardy, are not sufficiently ornamental to be worthy of cultivation, except in large collections. *L. racemosa* is the best of these, and is worthy of a place in the shrubbery: it is a hardy native plant.

THE CASSANDRA.

C. calyculata is a hardy shrub, very common in swamps. The foliage is rusty, and not ornamental;

and the chief merit of the plant is its expanding its flowers early in April. When well grown, it is very pretty; but it is not naturally of good habit. The flowers are pretty white bells.

There are varieties which differ only in height, size of flower, and breadth of leaf, respectively known as *nana*, *ventricosa*, and *latifolia*. All are of easiest culture in peat-soil.

Figured in Bot. Mag. t. 1286; Lodd. Cab. t. 1464, 530, and 1286.

THE ZENOBIA.

This plant, also known as *Andromeda speciosa*, is very showy and desirable, but is not hardy in the Northern States, as it is a native of Southern swamps. The flowers are large, white, and very showy; the foliage is deciduous.

The plants found in catalogues as *Andromeda pulverulenta*, *cassinæfolia*, *pulverulentissima*, *dealbata*, and *ovata*, are all varieties of this species, and like it are tender. They are very elegant and showy plants, and very desirable. In England they are hardy, and would probably prove so south of Philadelphia.

Figured in Lodd. Cab. t. 551; Bot. Mag. 25, t. 970, and 18, t. 667; Bot. Reg. 12, t. 1010.

THE ANDROMEDA.

The species to which this genus has been restricted by most botanists is *A. polifolia*, a charming little plant, with narrow, glaucous-green leaves and beautiful white flowers tipped with rosy-red.

It is a native of cold bogs of both continents, extending into high latitudes, and is therefore perfectly hardy.

The difficulty in cultivation is to keep it cool and damp. With us it grows and flowers beautifully in the shady part of a Rhododendron-bed on a northern hillside.

There are many varieties, differing in size of plant and color of flower: all thrive under the same treatment, and are desirable.

Figured in Bax. Brit. Bot. 5, p. 361 ; and in variety in Lodd. Cab. t, 546, 1591, 1714, 1725.

A. ROSMARINIFOLIA

Much resembles the last, and may be only a variety.

The plant found in catalogues as *Andromeda formosa* is a native of Nepal, and tender with us. The flowers are rosy-white, in drooping clusters, and very showy. Also called *Pieris formosa*.

ANDROMEDA MARIANA.

This species, also known as *Lyonia*, is a hardy plant, with deciduous foliage and large, white flowers. It is well worth growing, and does well in any good loamy soil.

Figured in Bot. Mag. t. 1597.

There are other native species, which are desirable in collections; but none of them are so showy as those we have mentioned.

The very beautiful *Andromeda floribunda* has been described under the genus *Leucothoe*.

THE DAPHNE.

Of this extensive genus, to which the well-known greenhouse plant *D. odora* belongs, but two are hardy in New England : one of these, *D. Mezereon*, is a common shrub in the spring garden, and produces its purple or white flowers with the early crocus. It is a very hardy plant, growing freely in good garden soil, and is ornamental in flower, foliage, and fruit. There is also an autumn-blooming variety.

DAPHNE CNEORUM

Is the most attractive of the hardy species. It is a low-growing plant, with evergreen foliage and terminal umbels of fragrant, pink flowers, which are produced in great profusion in early spring. Although indigenous to Central Europe, it is perfectly hardy with us, and is a most useful plant for low beds or for the borders of the shrubbery. The fragrance of the flowers is so strong as to be almost unpleasant in a close room, but in the garden they perfume the air delightfully. They open in sunny exposures in April, and, by a little care in having plants in different places, may be had in bloom far

into June : a second crop of flowers is sometimes
produced in September. The flowers vary somewhat
in shading, and there is said to be a white variety.

Variety MAJUS has larger flowers than the species,
and is a more desirable plant.

Variety VARIEGATUM has the foliage prettily edged
with yellow.

Figured in Bot. Mag. t. 313 ; Lodd. Cab. t. 1800.

D. altaica, a native of Siberia, and *D. alpina*,
from the Swiss Alps, both with white flowers, which
in the latter are fragrant, would probably prove
hardy; but we do not know of them in cultivation.

D. Laureola, the Spurge Laurel, indigenous to
most parts of Europe, is a good plant for shady
plantations, as it is not injured by the drip of trees.
It is not hardy in New England.

D. pontica, native of Asia Minor, and also found
in Siberia, is precariously hardy, and is killed in
exposed situations.

D. alpina is figured in Lodd. Cab. t. 66.

D. altaica in Bot. Mag. t. 1875 ; and in Lodd.
Cab. t. 399.

D. Laureola in Eng. Bot. 2, 119.

D. pontica in And. Rep. 2, t. 73 ; and Bot. Mag.
t. 1282.

THE SKIMMIA.

A genus of evergreen shrubs, from northern India
and Japan, of which one, *S. japonica*, is a very desir-

able plant. As its name implies, it is a native of Japan, and is a low-growing shrub found upon the mountains. The foliage is dark green, shining, and evergreen. The flowers are white, in long, clustered panicles on the ends of the branches, and are succeeded by bright, globular, scarlet berries. Altogether it is a very ornamental plant. With us it proves hardy in Rhododendron soil, and grows, flowers, and fruits freely.

Seedlings are easily raised from the berries.

Figured in Sieb. Fl. Jap. 68; Fl. des Serres, 7, p. 39; Bot. Mag. t. 4719; Illus. Hort. 1, t. 13.

SKIMMIA OBLATA.

This species, also from Japan, has large, rich, laurel-like foliage, and oblate berries of bright vermilion-red. It is a more showy plant than *S. japonica*, but we cannot vouch for its hardiness. As yet it is somewhat rare, but, as it grows readily from seed, will soon be common. The plant known as *S. fragrantissima* proves to be the male plant of this species, which is sometimes hermaphrodite, though usually unisexual.

Figured in The Florist, 1865, p. 161.

THE PERNETTYA.

These plants are pretty little, evergreen shrubs from South America. The foliage is small and very neat; the flowers little white bells, covering the plant, which are succeeded by pink berries. They

7

are more likely to be destroyed by the summer than by the winter; at least such has been our experience at Glen Ridge, where plants which survived two winters, with little injury, perished from the effects of the summer's sun. All the species are very impatient of the extremes of wet and dry, and if planted in full exposure to the rays of the sun soon perish, and an excess of moisture at the roots is sure to kill them. The best culture is to plant them in a Rhododendron-bed, with a northern exposure, and during winter to cover them lightly with pine-needles.

They are easily raised from seed.

The two species in cultivation are:—

P. MUCRONATA,

A native of the Straits of Magellan, with dark foliage, which contrasts well with the white flowers.

Figured in Bot. Reg. 20, t. 1675; and in Maud. Bot. 3, 112. And

P. ANGUSTIFOLIA,

A native of Chili. The foliage is dark, and the plant flowers very freely. This species seems quite as hardy as the preceding.

Figured in Bot. Reg. 26, t. 63; and in Bot. Mag. t. 3889.

There are other species which prove tender.

THE HYPERICUM.

The St. Johns-worts are well-known plants, with yellow flowers; some worthy of garden culture, and others mere weeds.

One species, however, is a very showy and desirable plant: —

HYPERICUM CALYCINUM

Is a native of Ireland, Scotland, and other parts of Europe, and proves perfectly hardy with us, if slightly protected during the winter. The foliage is large, evergreen, and thickly covered with pellucid dots; the flowers are large, yellow, and very showy, two or three inches in diameter, with reddish anthers. It is a low-growing shrub, thriving under the drip of trees, and well-calculated for banks, rockworks, or the margins of shrubberies. The roots are creeping, and a small plant will soon cover a large space.

Our plants are on the borders of a Rhododendron-bed, and are protected in winter by a slight covering of pine-needles. We do not regard this as necessary, for plants have done well wholly unprotected; but the foliage is very much browned and the beauty of the plant impaired.

Figured in Bot. Mag. t. 146; and in Eng. Bot. 29, t. 2017.

Of other species *H. Kalmianum* is a well-known inhabitant of our shrubberies, conspicuous for its yellow flowers in July; and *H. Uralum*, with us, a rather tender species from Nepal, with terminal corymbs of bright orange-yellow blossoms, is desirable.

Figured in Bot. Mag. t. 2375.

THE POLYGALA.

One species of this beautiful genus is suitable for cultivation with American plants: —

POLYGALA CHAMÆBUXUS

Is a dwarf-growing, evergreen, shrubby plant, with large, yellow flowers, a native of the Swiss and Austrian Alps. It is a neat, pretty plant, increasing rapidly from running roots, and freely producing its fragrant flowers during the spring and summer. We can scarcely regard it as perfectly hardy; but with a little care, covering the whole plant with pine-needles in winter, it may be preserved, and is well worth the trouble. Plants may be imported from England for about nine shillings per dozen.

They should be grown in a soil of peaty loam.

Figured in Bot. Mag. t. 316; and in Lodd. Cab. t. 593.

THE PYROLA.

Among the Wintergreens are some very pretty plants well worthy of cultivation. The common *Pyrola rotundifolia* is by no means an inelegant plant, and if not found wild is very desirable in the garden. The leaves are radical, smooth, roundish, and shining; the flowers white, delicately fragrant, drooping on a slender raceme.

It does well in any light, rich soil, and increases rapidly from its running roots : it prefers a rather moist, shady place. There are several varieties, differing in shape of the leaves and color of the flower.

P. elliptica closely resembles this species ; and *P. chlorantha, minor,* and *secunda,* are all neat-growing plants, thriving with little care, and worth growing in a collection.

MONESES UNIFLORA,

Formerly *Pyrola uniflora,* is not uncommon in northern woods. It is a delicate and very pretty plant, bearing one large, white or rosy, terminal flower, and increasing readily by creeping roots.

THE CHIMAPHILA.

These plants are low-growing herbs, with shining, evergreen foliage and jewelled flowers. The most common species is *C. umbellata,* sometimes called " Pipsissewa," or " Bitter-Sweet." The flowers are roes-colored, with purple anthers, and very pretty.

C. maculata, the other species, has lighter green leaves, marked with white ; and is a very showy, variegated-leaved plant.

It is not very common in New England, but recently we found it in great abundance on the slopes of the Alleghanies in Virginia. The flower is not so handsome as the last. All species do well in sandy loam and peat.

PART IV.

HERBACEOUS PLANTS ADAPTED FOR GROWTH
IN RHODODENDRON-BEDS.

PART IV.

HERBACEOUS PLANTS ADAPTED FOR GROWTH IN RHODODENDRON-BEDS.

————

THERE are many herbaceous plants, seldom found in good health in the garden, which thrive wonderfully if grown in Rhododendron-beds. Many of these are rare native plants, usually considered of difficult cultivation : but their only fault is refusing to grow under conditions in no way suited to their nature. To domesticate these choice wildlings, and to have them bloom under your own care in greater perfection than in their native haunts, is a triumph of floriculture which few achieve. Yet such success is not difficult, and a little study of the requirements of each plant will enable one to attain it.

Plants that naturally grow in the rich humus of old woods, rooting in the deep leaf-mould, or that find congenial soil in shady swamps, will not thrive transplanted to common garden soil and exposed in full sunshine.

For such and for many others the edges of Rhododendron-beds are suitable situations : they there
have moisture, depth of soil, and partial shade, and
seldom refuse to reward the grower.

We propose to enumerate a few of the plants that
have succeeded with us under such cultivation, in
the hope that others may repeat the experiment,
deriving therefrom a pleasure equal to our own.

THE HEPATICA.

Almost the first flower of spring, following hard
upon the snowdrop and bulbocodium, and often
opening before the crocus, — can there be a more
charming blossom ?

Pretty as our wild species is, the garden varieties
of the European type are far more showy; and
transplanted, in our cold and backward spring, are
true to their nature, blooming long before plants
born in our own woods unfold their delicate flowers.

Earliest of all is the double red Hepatica, perhaps the most charming of spring blossoms, a
sparkling little flower, already in bloom in sunny
spots when the early April days betoken spring, and
blooming on till May. Then follow our pretty single blue, pink, and white native varieties, with the
single red, the mauve (*H. Barlowii*), and the rare
white, with red stamens. Last, but no whit less
beautiful, comes the double blue; and that latest
acquisition, the Hungarian *H. angulosa*, with large,
deep-lobed leaves and sky-blue flowers, an inch in
diameter.

But where can we find all these? many will ask; and out of our own garden we should be at a loss where to seek for them. We know of no florist of this country who can supply an order; yet these plants should be grown by thousands, and be as cheap and as common as violets.

In England they are very cheap; and a few shillings will buy a dozen plants, well rooted in pots, and all ready to put out in the border. Like all spring-blooming plants, they should be imported in the autumn, wintered in a cold frame, and transplanted to the border in early spring.

If imported in spring, they usually make a rank growth in the cases, which perishes when the plants are set out; and, as no second growth is made, the plant dies.

For years we lost all our spring-imported plants; but since we have imported in autumn, it is seldom we lose a plant.

All the Hepaticas are natives of Europe and North America. They are low-growing plants, with evergreen, lobed leaves, and thrive well in any deep garden soil.

Our native varieties, transplanted from the woods, grow freely, and soon form large clumps.

All the varieties are worth growing. Had we to choose one, it would be the double red, as it has the most brilliant flowers, blooms earlier than the others, and more readily accommodates itself to various soils and exposures; but we should be loath to give up any.

The Hungarian *H. angulosa* is the largest species,

and a very showy plant: it proves hardy with us, and no choice collection should be without it.

Hepaticas do not require Rhododendron soil, but thrive wonderfully in the sunny edges of Rhododendron-beds, blooming gayly in early April, when the *Kalmia glauca*, the *Cassandra*, *Rhodora*, and Dauric Rhododendron begin to open their blossoms, and all the year are ornamental from their neat, evergreen foliage.

The only culture, when once planted, is to let them alone: they are impatient of disturbance and of extremes of drought and moisture.

In winter we lay an evergreen bough over the plants to protect the foliage from the sun, but this is not necessary. They are propagated by division in early spring.

To all we say, Grow hepaticas, even if the garden is but a few feet square. They occupy little room, and, are the sunniest, the brightest, the most cheery children of the floral world.

THE SANGUINARIA.

The Bloodroot (*S. canadensis*), a well-known native plant, thrives perfectly in the garden. Transplanted from the woods to a deep, rich soil, the flowers increase in size and in the number of petals, and ripen seed freely, which often sows itself.

It is curious to watch this plant in the early days of spring: a few hours will often be sufficient to expand the snowy blossoms, and to spread the countless yellow stamens to the sun.

The leaves, which at first enwrap the flower, grow very large, and protect the seed-pods until they ripen.

There is but one species, and there are no well defined varieties; though on some plants the flowers are larger than on others, and the stamens show a disposition to be converted into petals.

A sunny nook in the garden is well filled with this plant, which in deep, rich soil thrives without care, and blooms freely every spring.

THE JEFFERSONIA.

The only species, *J. diphylla*, bears a pretty white flower in early April, somewhat resembling that of the bloodroot. The leaves and foot-stalks are bluish-green, and the whole plant is glabrous: from the leaves folding together in two equal parts, the popular name "Twinleaf" is derived. The seed-capsule is very curious, opening by a hinged lid when the seed is ripe.

This is rather a rare plant, and is not found wild in New England. In cultivation, it grows freely in any good garden soil, and is easily propagated by division.

THE CALTHA.

Early in spring the bright yellow blossoms of the Marsh Marigold (*C. palustris*) are very conspicuous in wet meadows, and the leaves are sold in the markets as "water cresses." In cultivation, the plant is valuable as an early flower, and does not require a wet soil, but easily domesticates itself if planted in good loam.

The double variety, which is not uncommon, is very showy, lasting long in bloom, and is very brilliant in color.

C. parnassifolia and *radicans* are also pretty exotic species.

All are easily propagated by division.

The Dentaria.

The Toothworts are pretty little, spring-blooming plants, with delicate foliage and white or purple flowers. They are easily cultivated in rich loam, and, though rather inconspicuous, occupy little room, and take care of themselves. We have grown one species for years, in a sheltered nook of a Rhododendron-bed, and admire it the more each spring.

The species, which are *D. diphylla, lacinata, maxima, multifida,* and *heterophylla,* much resemble each other in flower.

Propagated by division in spring.

The Anemone.

All of the hardy species of these favorite plants thrive in Rhododendron soil. We have already described the Hepatica, which is only a sub-genus of Anemone, as one of the most desirable of spring flowers ; and many other species, although not such early bloomers, are most ornamental and attractive.

We are all familiar with the wild Anemone of our woods (*A. nemorosa*), varying in color from pure white to deep pink or purple, and tinted like some delicate sea-shell; but we have not all grown this charming flower in the garden, and watched it day by day, from the first moment the dark foliage breaks through the ground until the delicate blossom nods in the spring breezes. This is easy to do; for the plant does well in any light, rich loam, increasing rapidly by its slender root-stocks, and carpeting the ground with rich foliage, spangled with lovely blossoms. We have only to transplant it and let it alone, and year after year it will reward us with a profusion of blossoms. The double varieties, both white and pink, we have in our garden: both are very charming and attractive, and grow as freely as the species. An allied plant is the Rue-leaved Anemones (*A. thalictroides*, or *Thalictrum anemenoides*), found both in the single and double varieties, pure white, very showy, quite as easy to cultivate, and very desirable, not only for the flower, but also for the delicate foliage.

Anemone apennina, although a native of Italy, proves hardy with us; but we have been somewhat disappointed in its proving a very shy bloomer. The flowers are blue, and very showy.

The English *A. ranunculoides*, with yellow, buttercup-like flowers, is precariously hardy, and has not with us proved a satisfactory plant.

A. narcissiflora, a charming European species, is perfectly hardy, and produces its white flowers in great profusion.

A. pennsylvanica is a tall-growing species, blooming in summer, and, although a little coarse, is a
desirable plant. We prefer it, however, in good
garden soil, rather than in a Rhododendron-bed, as
it spreads rapidly and soon appropriates every thing
to itself.

The sub-genus, *Pulsatilla*, contains several species
of spring-blooming plants, with dull purple flowers:
in bloom they are not very showy, but the long-
tailed heads of seed are ornamental.

No species, however, can compare with the Japan
Anemone, and its hybrid Honorine Joubert, probably
a cross between *A. japonica* and the Nepalese *A. viti-
folia*. The species and a variety, *A. j. speciosa*,
have reddish-pink flowers in October, and are very
desirable autumn-blooming plants; but the hybrid is
the best flower of autumn. The foliage is large and
showy, deep green and of vigorous growth; the plant
tall; the flowers very large, pure white with yellow
centre, and produced in great abundance. It is
perfectly hardy, and easily propagated by division;
indeed, each little piece of the root will make a
plant.

We know of no more charming flower to place
here and there in open spots among Rhododendrons.
The flower shows well on the dark background of
foliage, and lends it an additional charm: from the
middle of September until cut off by late frosts the
plant is a mass of flower.

If we had only the genus Anemone to ornament
the spring garden, we might be content; for it contains many species, which vary greatly in appear-

ance. All are not hardy, but frame protection is sufficient to preserve them through the winter; and they well repay the trouble. Many hardy species are rarely found in cultivation in this country; but a few shillings will import a choice assortment from Europe, where both florists and amateurs fully appreciate the beauty of these charming plants.

THE CLAYTONIA.

Two of the species, *C. virginica* and *caroliniana*, are pretty, spring-blooming plants, which succeed well in any deep, rich soil. The root is a small tuber, from which in early spring a slender stem arises, bearing two leaves, and terminated by a raceme of delicate pink blossoms, deeply veined with darker shades.

Plants procured from the woods and once established take care of themselves, and increase both by root and seed.

THE SCILLA.

All the exotic Squills are better suited to the bulb border than the Rhododendron-bed, as they require rather a light and sandy soil.

The best is *S. sibirica*, with deep blue flowers in early spring: a plant which is worth every trouble to have in perfection.

A clump of this is in place anywhere in the garden, and it would be difficult to name a more sparkling floral gem.

The Squill of the western prairies, *S. Fraseri,* needs a deep, rich soil.

The flower is whitish-blue, and very pretty. It flowers freely, and once introduced needs no further care; and, if easily obtained, is well worth growing.

THE CAMASSIA.

The only species, *C. esculenta,* is a small bulbous plant, with leaves somewhat resembling a hyacinth, and a tall spike of a dozen or more showy purple flowers. It is, with us, a rare plant, though on our north-western coast it is so abundant as to form the chief food of the Indians. It succeeds in deep, rich soil, and flowers in May. Our plants were imported from England. It proves perfectly hardy.

THE OXALIS.

The common wild Oxalis of our northern woods (*O. Acetosella*), which often carpets the ground for miles, is familiar to all White Mountain tourists. It is a delicate little plant, pretty in foliage and its white, veined blossoms, and increases rapidly by its creeping root-stocks. It takes kindly to cultivation, and if placed in a congenial soil soon covers the ground.

There is, however, another species, rare in New England, which is a very beautiful plant, and quite as easy of domestication. *O. violacea* is a little bulb, with clover-like leaves and charming purple flowers.

None of the exotic species are prettier than this, and none more desirable. It is perfectly hardy, grows freely, and flowers profusely in the latter part of May.

THE ERYTHRONIUM.

The "Dog-tooth Violet," which is no violet at all, but rather a lily, is a very pretty, spring-blooming plant. The exotic species, in its many varieties, is showy both in foliage and flower. Our native species, though not so showy, are no less interesting. The most common are *E. americanum* and *E. albidum*, with yellow and white flowers respectively: the former is more showy both in foliage and flower. Both are small plants, with lily-like foliage, springing from small, deep-rooting bulbs, and bear handsome nodding flowers. They are a little capricious in cultivation, and seldom succeed in common garden soil. In the deep loam of the Rhododendron-bed they grow freely, and seldom fail to bloom.

The yellow species is very common, and may easily be procured; but the white-flowered must be sought on the western prairies.

THE ARISÆMA.

A. triphyllum, commonly known as "Jack in the Pulpit," or "Indian Turnip," is a common plant in rich, damp woods. It is curious in flower, ornamental in foliage, and very showy in fruit.

A place should be found for it in the garden, and no situation will suit it better than the rich, deep soil of a Rhododendron-bed, where it will also find congenial shade. In such a situation it will attain wonderful size, and seldom fail to ripen the showy scarlet fruit.

A. Dracontium, also hardy, is not so showy a species, but is worth growing in a collection.

There are many pretty exotic species, but none have proved hardy with us.

THE PACHYSANDRA.

This curious plant is of very easy culture, growing and flowering freely in any rich, damp soil.

The flowers are greenish or purplish white, and peculiarly scented. The foliage is coarse, deep green, perennial. For covering the surface, this plant is well adapted, though as especially ornamental it is not to be recommended.

The species is *P. procumbens*, a native of mountains in the Southern States, and perfectly hardy.

The variegated-leaved variety is very pretty, but seems somewhat more tender than the species.

THE DODECATHEON.

The " American Cowslip," or " Shooting Star," is not uncommon in gardens. It is a singularly elegant plant in the wild form, and some of the seedlings raised in cultivation are among the handsomest of spring flowers. It grows in any rich, moist soil, and is easily increased by seed or division. In color the flowers vary from white to deep red or purple. The species is *D. Meadia*.

A form from our north-western coast (*D. Jeffrey-anum*) is a far larger plant, with large, dark green foliage, and tall scapes of deep pink flowers.

THE TRIENTALIS.

A pretty little plant, with starry white blossoms, springing from the centre of a whorl of light green leaves, is the " Star Flower " (*T. americana*). It grows readily in any damp, rich soil, and if given a shady situation is well worth cultivating.

THE MITELLA.

No better plant for covering the surface of the ground can be found than the common Mitella (*M. diphylla*). The foliage, though not especially showy, is neat; and the racemes of delicate white flowers are very elegant.

The plant blooms freely, spreads rapidly, and requires no care.

M. nuda is a very small species, with delicate greenish flowers.

THE TIARELLA.

This plant (*T. cordifolia*) is not so showy as the Mitella, which it much resembles, but is equally useful as a low-spreading plant. The flowers are white.

Both this and the Mitella are easily obtained from the woods, and soon adapt themselves to cultivation.

THE HELONIAS.

H. bullata is a very rare and beautiful native plant, growing naturally in damp meadows, and thriving in cultivation in any deep, moist soil. The leaves are lanceolate, radical, spreading flat on the ground, evergreen. The flowers are clustered on a tall spike, and are of a purplish-pink, turning green as they fade. It is a flower seldom seen in cultivation, and finds a congenial soil in a Rhododendron-bed, where it will flower freely every spring.

THE CLINTONIA.

The large, shining leaves of *Clintonia borealis* are very conspicuous in low woods. The flower is greenish, and on examination very pretty; but the berry, which is bright blue, is, after the foliage, the most attractive part of the plant.

There is no difficulty in cultivating this plant, as it grows rapidly, and with us flowers more freely than in the wild state. The foliage is strikingly handsome, and this alone should entitle it to cultivation.

C. umbellata is a rarer species, with white flowers speckled with green or purplish dots, which we have not seen.

THE CORNUS.

C. canadensis, the " Bunch-berry " of our northern woods, is another plant more charming in fruit

than in flower. The root is woody; the flowers, or
rather floral involucre, greenish-white: the berries
brilliant scarlet, and very showy. This plant does
well in any good, rich soil, and flowers freely; but
with us fails to set its berries, for which, as yet, we
have not been able to discover a reason. It is worth
growing, however, for the flowers alone.

Easily obtained from the woods.

THE CONVALLARIA.

The Lily of the Valley (*C. majalis*) is too well
known to require description, and we need use no
argument to find a place for it in the flower garden.
It is in place everywhere, in beds by itself, rambling
through the grass, or carpeting the ground under
trees. For delicacy, beauty, and fragrance, it has no
superior. In a Rhododendron-bed there is danger
of its growing too luxuriantly and injuring the other
plants, but if kept within bounds it may be used
with good effect. When it sets its scarlet berries it
is very showy.

The varieties with double flowers, and with single
and double rose-colored flowers, are only desirable
in a collection: in the latter the color is a dirty
pink, and not attractive; all are, however, very
fragrant.

The variegated-leaved kinds, especially that with
golden-striped foliage, are very handsome, but are
not common. They are well worth growing, as the
variegation is handsome and permanent.

The Solomon's Seal (*Polygonatum*), and (*Smilacina*), and the Bellworts (*Uvularia*) are all very

pretty plants, and should find place in the garden if possible. The best for surface covering is *Smilacina bifolia*, with shining foliage, fragrant, white flowers, and red berries. All these are readily obtained from the woods.

The Ficaria.

This genus is closely allied to Ranunculus, indeed by some is combined with it. The flowers of the common species, *F. ranunculoides*, greatly resemble small buttercups ; but they open only in sunshine, and bloom earlier in the spring. The roots are small tubers, from which spring glossy green leaves, followed by the bright flowers in early May. In a few weeks the foliage fades and dies away, and the plant disappears until the next spring. The double variety is a rarer and more showy plant, and the white-flowered variety is seldom found. All are well worth growing, and increase rapidly by multiplication of the tubers. They only require common garden soil.

The Ranunculus.

Of the Buttercups the only one we can recommend for a choice collection is the " Fair Maids of France " (*R. aconitifolius flore pleno*).

It is a delicate plant, with fine-cut foliage and pretty double, white flowers. Although not uncommon, it has an ugly way of dying out, and is one of those plants which, unless great care is taken, is often lost. It should be grown in rich, damp soil, and not be allowed to dry up.

THE HELLEBORE.

The best of the Hellebores is the " Christmas Rose" (*H. niger*), a plant by no means so well known as its merits deserve. It is the best winter flower we have; and by covering the plant with a cold frame, to keep the snow from crushing it, may be gathered any day from November to April. It is attractive both in foliage and flower: the former is large, deep-cut, dark shining evergreen; the latter measure from one to two inches in diameter, are white, often tinged with pink, single, and full of bright golden stamens.

Cold has no effect upon them: if frozen hard, they thaw out uninjured. The plant is perennial, and requires a deep, moist soil, where it will not dry up in summer.

When once planted, it should not be disturbed, as it does not transplant readily, and takes long to become well established.

H. fœtidus, a native of England, is showy in foliage and flower, but with us has not proved hardy.

H. viridis, which much resembles it, but is a smaller plant, is hardy, and is naturalized in some parts of the country.

H. olympicus is a beautiful species from India, with pinkish flowers, figured in Bot. Reg. 28, t. 58. It is not quite hardy, but by covering the plants with a frame we winter them successfully.

H. atrorubens and *odorus*, natives of Hungary, are also a little tender.

Figured in Bot. Mag. t. 4581.

H. orientalis is tender even with frame protection.

THE EPIMEDIUM.

We consider this one of the most elegant plants in our spring garden; and no one who has seen the showy and curious blossoms of *E. macranthum* and *violaceum* will dispute the assertion. The foliage is very neat, finely toothed, and remains in full beauty all summer; the flowers, which are freely produced in May, are singularly graceful. No description can give an idea of them. All the species are hardy perennials, and do well in any deep garden loam, but succeed far better in the moist, rich soil of a Rhododendron-bed, where we grow them in great perfection. Of some twenty species the best are *macranthum*, *pinnatum*, *diphyllum*, with white flowers, and *violaceum*, with white and purple flowers; all natives of Japan.

E. alpinum is a European species, with reddish-yellow flowers, which increases rapidly, and is a good plant for covering the ground in shady places, or under trees : it also thrives well on rock-work. All the species are propagated by division; but they are impatient of disturbance, and should be removed only when absolutely necessary, as they always are some years in recovering from the effect. The larger the clumps are the better, and the more showy are they in foliage and flower.

THE CYPRIPEDIUM.

This well-known genus of terrestrial orchids, commonly called Lady's Slipper, find their congenial home in a Rhododendron-bed; and only in such soil can they be cultivated in perfection.

The different species are among the most beautiful of our native plants; while their easy culture, the one requirement of soil being attended to, should place them among the most popular of garden flowers.

Yet they are very seldom grown, and outside of our own garden we know of none where all the indigenous hardy species can be found in cultivation.

The most common eastern species is *C. acaule* or *humile*, usually found wild in dry sandy woods, producing its showy pink or purplish flowers in May. This species is rather difficult to domesticate; but we have succeeded, by giving it a more sandy soil than the other species, removing it from the woods both in early spring just as growth was beginning, and in autumn when the plant was at rest.

A variety with white flowers is rarely found.

C. arietinum, the Ram's Head, is the rarest species, so rare, indeed, that many amateurs have never seen it in bloom. It is a small plant, with flowers which need close examination to reveal their beauties: the lip is veined red and white, the petals greenish-brown. It is a native of cold bogs, and if allowed to dry up in cultivation seldom survives.

A shady spot in rich, damp soil is the place for it.

C. parviflorum and *pubescens*, the smaller and larger yellow Lady's Slipper, are very showy plants, and the easiest to cultivate. If placed in good soil, with an admixture of peat and sand, they increase rapidly, and soon form large clumps. In bloom they are very showy, often giving two, and sometimes three flowers on a stem. Although usually considered species, they seem to run into each other. These plants will live in common garden soil, but they die out in a few years.

C. calceolus is a European species, with yellow flowers, which proves with us perfectly hardy, and is a very desirable plant.

Next to the Ram's Head, the smallest species is the white-flowered Lady's Slipper of the West (*C. candidum*). It is a very pretty plant, with delicate white flowers, the lip looking like a bird's egg.

It flowers very freely, and takes kindly to cultivation.

By far the finest species is *C. spectabile*, a native of our northern woods, and one of the most showy of our native plants.

It is a tall plant, growing from eighteen inches to two feet high, with large clasping foliage, and beautiful white flowers, blotched in front with pinkish-purple: there is also a pure white variety. In good soil it becomes a very conspicuous plant, giving from one to three flowers on a stem, and soon increasing so as to form a large clump. It blooms in July, long after the other species have faded.

All the Lady's Slippers continue long in bloom,

and are very ornamental: we cannot have too many of them.

The best way to obtain a stock is from the woods, for generally florists cannot supply them.

They may be transplanted early in the spring or late in the autumn, and once planted should be seldom disturbed.

THE TRILLIUM.

All the species are low-growing plants, with tuberous roots or root-stalks, and are remarkable for having all the parts of the plant in threes. They come up in very early spring, blossom, and die away in a few weeks, unless they set seed. The finest species is *T. grandiflorum*, a very beautiful plant, which succeeds better in cultivation than most of our indigenous flowers.

The individual blossoms are pure white, changing to deep rose before they fade, and in rich soils are often more than two inches in diameter.

A clump of this plant is one of the most attractive objects in the spring garden.

T. erectum, a more common species, is a very showy plant: the flowers are dark chocolate-color. There is also a variety with dirty white flowers.

T. sessile, a western species, has also dull-colored blossoms, but is very showy from the elegant foliage, which is beautifully marbled with light and dark green.

T. pictum or *erythrocarpum* is the "Painted Trillium," and is the most difficult of all to cultivate.

It grows best in pure peat, and needs a very shady situation.

The flowers are white, delicately painted with rich lake at the base of each petal.

T. cernuum, the "Nodding Trillium," our most common species, has small pinkish-white flowers, which nod beneath the leaves. It is not very showy, and will grow in any garden soil.

There are also some Southern species.

All the Trilliums do best in rich, deep, peaty loam: they are increased by seed or division, but are somewhat impatient of removal. They should be transplanted from the woods in early spring, and soon domesticate themselves.

THE LILY.

All the Lilies like a deep, rich soil, except perhaps our wild blackberry lily, which thrives in dry sandy loam; but some never display themselves in full beauty except in a soil in which peat has been mixed.

This is especially the case with two of our native species, *L. superbum* and *canadense*, the drooping-flowered lilies of the fields, which naturally grow in rich meadows. These, removed to a Rhododendron-bed, become plants of wonderful beauty. During the last summer, we had about thirty specimens of these species, not one of which was less than five feet in height, each stalk giving from ten to thirty drooping flowers. The effect of these, rising from the rich foliage of the Rhododendrons, was very fine. The variety of color — for even of the same species no two plants are alike in shading — was also very pleasing.

Another species, which is never seen in full beauty unless planted in Rhododendron soil, is the Purple Martagon. This past year bulbs of this kind, two years planted, threw up stalks over four feet in height, which produced from twenty to thirty flowers each.

L. Catesbæi, the Southern Red Lily, also grows and blooms very freely, as do also all the varieties of *L. umbellatum, aurantium*, and *croceum*. The noble *L. auratum* seems to thrive better in a soil of peat, loam, and sand ; and we had, the last summer, stalks an inch in diameter and four feet high, the largest giving seventeen flowers from bulbs two years planted.

The Japan Lilies, while blooming in the Rhododendron-bed, do not, however, exhibit any remarkable luxuriance. They are, however, very effective, as the background of dark evergreen foliage sets off the large, white flowers to great advantage.

The same may be said of the beautiful Long-flowered Lily (*L. longiflorum*) and the Scarlet Martagon (*L. chalcidonicum*) ; indeed the latter does not succeed in peat.

The old white Lily (*L. candidum*) seems also to prefer a lighter and more sandy soil.

Some of the rarer species, such as *L. tenuifolium, pumilum*, and *kamtschaticum*, are very showy planted on the borders of Rhododendron-beds.

The old Tiger Lily also does well, but is rather coarse, and better adapted for the shrubbery.

There are no better plants than Lilies to mingle with Rhododendrons: generally sparse in foliage, the latter supply it; and the showy flowers are more effective than when wholly unrelieved by green, as we usually see them.

They grow freely, and once planted take care of themselves. Indeed, a Rhododendron-bed is worth all the trouble of making, if only to show the perfection to which our native Lilies can be grown.

INDEX.

INDEX.

8*

Cambridge: Press of John Wilson and Son.

www.ingramcontent.com/pod-product-compliance
Lightning Source LLC
Chambersburg PA
CBHW020623030726
47497CB00007B/2388